"You have my word,"

Marina said solemnly. At home, that would have been enough.

"I need more than that," Andrew said. "As it happens, I've got some time on my hands, and I might as well spend it keeping my eye on you."

She shrugged, hoping to convey the impression that his attention meant very little to her. "As you wish."

Her lack of concern didn't fool him. He grinned almost wolfishly as he took a step toward her. "I think I should warn you that there's nothing I like better than solving puzzles."

"Surely," she murmured, "your work provides you with enough of those."

"I've always thought so. Until now." He was closer still, his breath warm on her cheek, his hands infinitely gentle as they stroked lightly up and down her arms. "I can't decide whether you're deliberately being mysterious, or whether there's something you genuinely feel you have to hide. But either way, I intend to find out."

Maura Seger was prompted by a love of books and a vivid imagination to decide, at age twelve, to be a writer. Twenty years later her first book was published. So much, she says, for overnight success! Now each book is an adventure, filled with fascinating people who always surprise her.

MAURA SEGER

SEA GATE

Published by Silhouette Books
America's Publisher of Contemporary Romance

SILHOUETTE BOOKS

ISBN 0-373-51172-8

SEA GATE

Copyright © 1987 by Maura Seger.

All rights reserved. Except for use in any review, the reproduction or utilization of this work in whole or in part in any form by any electronic, mechanical or other means, now known or hereafter invented, including xerography, photocopying and recording, or in any information storage or retrieval system, is forbidden without the written permission of the editorial office, Silhouette Books, 300 East 42nd Street, New York, NY 10017 U.S.A.

All characters in this book have no existence outside the imagination of the author and have no relation whatsoever to anyone bearing the same name or names. They are not even distantly inspired by any individual known or unknown to the author, and all incidents are pure invention.

This edition published by arrangement with Harlequin Books S.A.

® and TM are trademarks of Harlequin Books S.A., used under license. Trademarks indicated with ® are registered in the United States Patent and Trademark Office, the Canadian Trade Marks Office and in other countries.

Visit Silhouette at www.eHarlequin.com

Printed in U.S.A.

Prologue

The child heard the sound first. He lay in the darkness of his bedroom, his eyes wide open, looking up at the ceiling. A moment before he had been asleep, his favorite blanket clutched in his hand and his thumb securely in his mouth. He had not moved, except to open his eyes.

It did not occur to him to be afraid. He knew that his father was asleep in the next room and that he had only to call out to bring him to his side. He knew this in the same way that he knew the sun rose each morning and set at night, without having to think about it.

On the dresser near the bed there was a night-light in the shape of a lamb. The boy craned his neck slightly and looked at it. As he watched, the lamb's painted face changed. It smiled.

"Billy..." The sound came again, only clearer now. His name.

Without hesitation, he took his thumb out of his

mouth and, trailing his blanket, climbed out of the bed. His father had left the door to his bedroom open slightly. He slipped through it and padded down the hallway toward the back door.

He was three years old, and tall for his age. Standing on tiptoe, he was able to reach the latch and undo it. Beyond the door was a flagstone patio. There he paused, taking in the night smells, the rustle of the wind in the palm trees, the way everything looked different in the absence of day. Earlier there had been a bad storm that had left branches down across the expanse of lawn beyond the patio. The last remnants of it were passing overhead, clouds skittering before a freshening wind.

"Billy…" More urgent, calling him. A woman's voice, like the mother he remembered only in his dreams.

His father had told him never to go down to the beach alone. That was a hard and fast rule, and the one time he had even begun to disobey it, he had been spanked. The memory of that lingered and made him hesitate. Until the voice called again.

The sand was warm under his feet. He had walked the path many times with his father, or with Hildy, who looked after them, and even in darkness he knew his way. The rhythmic pulse of the surf grew stronger. He could see the foam-crested waves rolling onto the beach, turning it to gleaming silver.

Near the waves the sand was deeper. His feet sank into it, toes wiggling. Holding his blanket, thumb once again in his mouth, he looked around. Some little distance down the beach, a dark shape lay. Slowly, his lower lip sucked in and his eyes wide, he approached it.

Chapter 1

"I have no idea who she is," Andrew Paxton said into the phone. "I found her on the beach below my house last night. Or, more correctly, Billy found her."

He listened for a moment, his face grim. He was a tall, leanly built man whose naturally brown hair had long since been turned to amber blond by frequent exposure to the sun. His strong, assertive features were tanned and had a weather-beaten look to them. Fine lines radiated from around his dark brown eyes. He looked his age, thirty-four, and perhaps slightly more, as though the years had not been particularly kind to him.

"No," he said with a strained effort at patience, "of course he wasn't supposed to be out alone at that hour. He's not allowed on the beach by himself at any time. But he went, and he found her. She seems to be all right so far as I can tell. There's no sign of any serious injury, and she's sleeping peacefully."

Silence again as he listened to the man on the other end of the phone. His big body, clad in jeans and a knit shirt, stirred restively. He shouldn't have mentioned the woman during what would otherwise have been a routine call. The man in Washington—his name was David Longfellow—called once a week, regular as clockwork, more often if he thought there was any need. Andrew had long ago given up resenting his scrutiny. He took it for what it was, standard operating procedure, and let it go at that.

"Yes," he said. "I considered calling the authorities, but have you got any idea how busy they are? That storm did serious damage all across the island. Besides, as I said, she doesn't seem to need medical help, only rest."

He was confident in that judgment based on skills acquired as a medic in Vietnam a lifetime ago. Since then he had come home, returned to school, earned a doctorate in physics, married, had a son and lost a wife. Enough for several lifetimes; too much, he sometimes thought.

He was tired, and that fatigue roughened his voice. His patience was strained, not only by the man at the other end of the phone and his constant concerns about security, but more importantly by his worry over his son. It wasn't like Billy to disobey him. He would have to be punished, but Andrew was dreading doing that, even though it would be for the boy's own good. Punishing Billy was no different, worse even, than punishing himself.

"Look," he said abruptly, having decided that he'd given Longfellow enough of his time and attention, "I'll handle it. If there's any problem, I'll let you know. Good enough?"

The question was perfunctory at best. He hung up a few moments later and immediately put the security man out of his mind. There were far more important matters for him to attend to.

The woman, for one. She had been asleep for twelve hours, and he hadn't checked on her in the last two of those. Going silently to the door of the guest room, he opened it a crack and looked inside. The curtains he had drawn blocked out the bright afternoon sun. In the aftermath of the storm, the sky above Angle Key was a brilliant blue. Only wisps of stray clouds lingered at the horizon, faint remnants of the hurricane that had remained far distant from the American Virgin Islands, merely brushing them in passing. That had been enough; as he had told Longfellow, the authorities would be cleaning up for some time to come. Meanwhile, he had the woman to deal with.

Who the hell was she? He entered the room and closed the door behind him, then walked over to the bed and looked down at her. She lay exactly as he had left her two hours before, turned on her side under the sheet, a slender hand resting on the pillow near her face. She was breathing slowly and evenly, and her color had improved. She was no longer quite so pale, though he had to admit that her skin tone was unusual, appearing as it did to have had little exposure to the sun.

Most women her age got at least some tan, even if they were careful to avoid overexposure. Not even a new arrival from the mainland would have had skin of such luminous alabaster that it almost seemed to radiate light. With her waist-length hair a shade of ebony so dark as to have almost blue highlights, she would have been startling under any circumstances. That she was also perfectly formed from the top of her head to the bottom of her feet only added to the effect.

Andrew was well acquainted with that perfection, since it was he who had undressed her and put her to bed. In his initial concern for her, he had been impersonal in his examination. Only when he was convinced that she had no serious injuries had he allowed himself to appreciate the beauty before him. Whoever she was, she was unforgettable; it therefore stood to reason that someone, if not several someones, was looking for her.

Without pausing to think about what he was doing, he bent forward and very lightly touched her hair. It was dry, finally. He had toweled it as best he could the night before and left it spread out over the pillow. Although it was badly tangled, he could see that it was not absolutely straight but instead rippled like the tiny waves that on calm days washed against the beach below his house.

The faintly bemused stare with which he had been studying her gave way to a frown as he considered how fortunate she was to have survived the storm. As soon as it was light he had left Billy in the house with strict orders not to leave and gone down to the beach for any clue as to how his mysterious guest had gotten there. He had half expected to find the remnants of a destroyed boat and perhaps even evidence of further tragedy, but instead there had been nothing, not even a life jacket to indicate where she might have come from.

It would be left to the woman herself to tell him that, which she couldn't do until she woke up. Aware that he was still touching her hair, as though to urge her back into consciousness, he withdrew his hand. After the tremendous shock she must have gone through, she had to rest; nothing was more important than that.

Leaving the room, he cast her a glance over his shoulder and was reassured that she continued to sleep peacefully. The longer she did, the sooner she would be able to answer his questions, which were growing more numerous by the hour.

Billy was seated in front of the television set in the den. Instead of the cartoon show Andrew had last seen him watching, he had flipped to another channel that was broadcasting a documentary on undersea life. Sitting cross-legged, holding his blanket with his thumb firmly in his mouth, he appeared to be fascinated.

Andrew sat down on the floor beside him and put an arm around his shoulders. Billy looked up and smiled. "She sleepin'."

It wasn't a question; he seemed perfectly well aware that the woman he had found was all right. His father had taken some pains to assure him of that, once he was sure of it himself. But Billy had needed little convincing. He had merely nodded and gone off to bed, apparently not even concerned that he was going to be punished for what he had done.

His father stifled a sigh. Gently he said, "We have to talk, young man."

Billy had turned his attention back to the program. He continued to stare at it as he asked, "Wha' 'bout?" The thumb in his mouth muffled his words slightly, but they were still perfectly comprehensible. He had said his first word at seven months and had been talking ever since. Andrew enjoyed nothing as much as conversations with his son, but this one was going to be difficult.

"You know you weren't supposed to go down to the beach alone."

Billy shot him a surprised look. "Had to go."

Whatever his father had been expecting, that wasn't it. Billy seemed to think that no further explanation was necessary, but Andrew disagreed. "What do you mean, you had to?"

"She called me."

"She? The woman?"

Billy frowned. It was the look his father knew meant that he was trying to work something out in his own mind. Billy forgot about the television and turned his attention fully to Andrew. His small brow knitted further as he said, "She. Momma."

Andrew jerked slightly in surprise. His son had no qualms about mentioning his mother; in fact, he enjoyed looking at photographs of her and talking about her. But to bring her up in this context made no sense.

"Billy…you know Momma had to go away."

His son nodded solemnly. "Went to heaven."

"That's right. Perhaps you were dreaming about her…."

"No," Billy said firmly. "Heard her. She called me."

"Your mother did?"

"The woman." He shrugged his small shoulders, recognizing the contradiction in what he said, but unable to reconcile it. Rather than try, he went back to his program.

Andrew stared at him for a moment. Billy seemed perfectly happy, which in the final analysis was what mattered. If he had somehow confused the woman in the guest room with his mother, they would simply have to work that out. He supposed it was natural enough, since the boy was at an age when all women appealed to him as potential mothers. That had placed his father in some interesting situations from which he had become adept at extricating himself.

It wasn't that he had no thought of marrying again, although in the first year after Elizabeth's death he wouldn't have believed it possible he would ever get over her. The fact was that time had proven, as always, to be a great healer. There had even been one or two women with whom he might have forged more lasting relationships had not his commitments to Billy and his work intervened.

Above all, Billy came first. After two and a half years of single parenthood, he felt that he was a better-than-average father, mainly because he worked hard at it. But any parent, no matter how good, could make mistakes occasionally. He might be on the verge of making one now, but he couldn't seem to help it.

He was going to forget about the episode on the beach. He would watch Billy more carefully and make sure that when Hildy returned from looking after her sick sister, she would do the same. But he wouldn't punish him for the action that had in all likelihood saved a life.

Greatly relieved by his decision, he sat back to enjoy the program with his son. They were watching Jacques Cousteau describe the life cycle of coral beds when a slight sound from the door alerted Andrew. He turned, and a shock roared through him.

He had known she was beautiful, but that still hadn't prepared him for the effect of such beauty when it was animated by consciousness. Asleep she had been breathtaking; awake she was stunning, and not in the least because she was nude.

Billy looked at her with friendly interest. He had been taught to feel no shame about the human body and felt none now. "'Lo," he said, going so far as to remove his thumb from his mouth.

The woman smiled, a bit uncertainly, Andrew thought, as well she might, considering her lack of apparel. He stood up and went to her, reaching as he did so for the afghan tossed over the couch. Absently he noticed that his hands shook as he wrapped it around her.

"You must still be in shock," he said; then, thinking that she might be very worried about where she was and what had happened to her, he went on. "There's nothing to be afraid of. You had a bad experience but you're all right. This is Angle Key. I'm Andrew Paxton, and this is my son, Billy. You were washed up on the beach below our house."

The woman watched him carefully as he spoke. She seemed to be struggling to understand what he said, and he wondered for a moment if he might have made a mistake: perhaps she had a concussion or an injury of some other sort.

A moment later he decided that was not the case. She was confused, understandably enough, but capable of comprehending what he said. "Paxton," she repeated with a slight accent he couldn't place. Her voice was soft and melodious. She looked at him directly as she spoke, and he was struck by the clarity of her sea-green eyes. They seemed to see directly into his soul.

She smiled, and a dimple appeared at the corner of her mouth. He was aware of a tightness in his chest, and elsewhere, that was growing steadily more noticeable. With a considerable effort of will, he wrenched his thoughts from their carnal path.

Billy had stood up and come to their side. He reached out a hand, and the woman took it. She held the afghan with the other. It had slipped off her shoulders and down far enough to reveal the high, full curve of her breasts. Her state of undress seemed to cause her no concern. She smiled at Billy, who gazed back at her as though enraptured.

Andrew cleared his throat. "Perhaps you'd like to sit down, Miss…"

She gave him a quizzical look. "Miss?"

"Your name," he prompted, wondering if she could be slow-witted. It didn't seem right that anyone so physically perfect could be damaged in any way, yet the possibility existed. He preferred to believe that she was still feeling the effects of her experience, and repeated himself gently.

"Oh, yes," she said as she lowered herself onto the couch with Billy beside her. Her bare legs were long and slender; Andrew's unimpeded view halfway up her thighs reminded him of that. Even her feet were lovely. He made another effort to place her accent, if only to distract himself, but without success.

"My name is Marina," she said. "Marina Lirularia."

Her name sounded vaguely European, as did her accent, though not enough that he could say with any certainty where she might have come from. "Are you visiting near here?" he asked.

Again she hesitated before answering, as though she was translating the question into another language. "Not exactly.… I was…at sea."

"On a yacht?" She gave him a baffled look, as though she didn't understand the word. "Were you on a boat?" he asked.

"Boat, yes. A…sort of boat. At sea."

That didn't tell him much, but it was more than he

had known before. A boat might mean other people in need of help. "How big a boat?"

She smiled and shook her head. "Not big…small."

"Were you alone? I'm only asking in case the authorities should be notified. You might have friends in trouble."

Quickly she assured him that she didn't. "One person only. Me. No author—" She stumbled over the word. "Authorities."

"You were by yourself, then. That's something, at least, though I'm afraid that your boat must have been completely destroyed."

A look of regret flashed across her lovely face. "Yes, I think so, too."

"But don't worry. You can call home and get whatever you need: credit cards, clothes—" He broke off, aware that her slanted eyebrows were knitting together. "Is something wrong?"

Bare shoulders shrugged enticingly. "There is no one I can call."

"But surely you must have some family."

She sighed and leaned back against the couch. "Yes, of course, but they are…out of touch."

"What about friends then?"

"I'm afraid…the same. But," she assured him, seeing his concern, "I will manage."

"Like hell! I'm sorry, but I don't see how you expect to. You've got no identification—I checked when I undressed you—and no money. Without either, you're not going to get very far."

If he had thought, belatedly, that she might be embarrassed by his reference to undressing her, he needn't have worried. She merely smiled again. "Thank you for helping me. Your assistance is very appreciated."

"I'd do the same for anyone in that state," he said, oddly put out by her formality. He didn't want her treating him like a stranger to be kept at arm's length, even though he was fully aware that she had a perfect right to do so.

Their eyes met, and he was struck once more by the unusual color of hers. Her lids dropped slightly, but not before he glimpsed what he thought was concern and even a touch of fear. That was quickly denied as she said, "I have imposed on you long enough. If I could have my clothes..."

She had been clad only in a silky tunic, mid-thigh in length, a tiny scrap of panties and a pair of sandals. He remembered wondering if she had been attending a costume party. "They were pretty well wrecked," he said.

Marina fingered the afghan. "I suppose I have to wear something."

"That would probably be for the best," Andrew said dryly. "I'll see what I can find for you." He stood up hastily, not wishing to entertain visions of her unclad any longer than he had to, and left the room. When he returned a short time later, Billy and Marina were still seated on the couch. They were talking together and seemed to be playing some sort of game, which they broke off at his approach.

"You should be able to manage with these," he said, handing her a shirt and jeans. There were also a pair of beach thongs and a hairbrush. It wasn't much, but at least it would do until they could go shopping. That he would have to buy her some clothes did not disturb him. But the thought that by doing so he would be making it possible for her to leave did.

Marina was staring at the clothes in bewilderment.

She turned the small pile this way and that, peering at it uncertainly.

"They're mine," Andrew explained. "Our housekeeper's wouldn't fit you." Thinking of Marina draped in Hildy's voluminous garments made him smile. "She's on the large side. Of course, I am, too. But you can roll up the sleeves and cuffs."

She still didn't seem to get the idea, so he reached over and demonstrated, rolling up one sleeve of the shirt. "See? That way they won't bag quite so much."

Marina nodded slowly. She seemed at a loss as to what to do next. It occurred to Andrew that he had no idea when she had last eaten. Hunger might well account for her air of confusion.

Gently he led her out of the den and down the hall to the guest room. "There's the bathroom," he said. "When you're done, we'll be in the kitchen fixing dinner."

"Hot dogs," Billy chirped. "Baked beans an' soda pop."

"I think we can do a bit better than that. Come on, then." With a hand on his son's shoulder, he steered him out of the room and shut the door behind them.

Chapter 2

Marina stood staring at the closed door for several moments before she slowly turned and looked around the bathroom. It was fitted with light blue fixtures whose purpose she could, with a small effort, define. The floor was covered with a thick carpet of royal blue that tickled her bare toes; the walls were made of white tile decorated at the corners with small flowers in shades of blue and yellow that matched the fluffy towels hung on a rack.

A curtained window looked out over a garden, and beyond that she could glimpse the sea lapping at the beach. Her throat tightened as she jerked her gaze away. It would do no good to give in to her fears. Her safety depended on remaining calm and not losing control.

Which was easier said than done. Never in her life had she felt so completely alone. It was her own fault, of course, but that didn't make it any easier to bear.

The risks she had so blithely dismissed when she set out on her adventure had turned starkly real and unavoidable. Since first realizing that her craft was in serious trouble, she had known that she might never see home again. Not unless she was very clever and very lucky.

Luck, at least, seemed already to have been granted her. She dropped the afghan and looked at herself carefully, reassuring herself that she wasn't injured. A few bruises shone against the paleness of her skin, but there was nothing that would cause her any problem. Her situation was another matter.

The man puzzled her. He seemed kind, and, indeed, the care he had given her confirmed that. She had felt his desire for her and wondered if that might somehow be related to her nudity. There was so much she didn't understand.

Her ignorance rankled. It had been the spur that sent her on her ill-fated journey, and now it troubled her more than ever. At any moment she was likely to say or do something that would give herself away.

She picked up the hairbrush, examined it for a moment, then began to rid her hair of its tangles, thinking all the while of how she might handle the problem of her identity. The man was intelligent; the strength and subtlety of his mind were as clear to her as his height and breadth. He would not be easy to fool.

With a sigh, she laid the brush on the counter, deciding that she had done the best she could with her hair. It fell in thick waves over her shoulders and down her back. She pulled it out from beneath the shirt, which she managed, after a few fumbled attempts, to button. The pants proved more difficult; fortunately, she had noticed the man wearing them and therefore had some idea of how to put them on, but whether they fastened in the front or the back she could not remember. Finally deciding that the front was more comfortable, she grinned in triumph when she figured out how the zipper worked. They sagged down around her slender hips, but by folding the waistband over several times she managed to keep them in place.

Having conquered the small but reassuring business of dressing herself, she felt better able to confront whatever might lie ahead. Her host had mentioned something about dinner, which was fortunate, since she was ravenously hungry. She took a last glimpse in the mirror, assured herself that she was indeed whole and alive, and left the room.

This time her sandals slapping against the tiled floor alerted Andrew that she was coming. He was standing at a counter, chopping vegetables for a salad. Billy perched on a stool beside him. They both looked up as she entered.

"Nice," Billy said, and smiled.

His father was less forthcoming. He thought she looked like a waif in the oversize clothes, a dangerously beautiful, seductive waif. Someone in need of protecting, even from himself.

"Sit down," he said, gesturing to the stool next to Billy. "We're having steak and salad. I hope that's all right."

The question was perfunctory; he really didn't expect her to object. Marina glanced at the slabs of red meat laid out on a platter beside the stove and frowned. They were much the same color and consistency as a particular sort of tuna she enjoyed, but her sensitive sense of smell told her they were from a very different source. She swallowed hastily and managed a bright smile. "They look delicious."

"They will be," Andrew said. "After they're cooked."

At least some sort of preparation was involved, which might render them more palatable. In the meantime, she wasn't going to worry about it. "May I help?" she asked politely, unsure of the proper etiquette. She had never before seen a man prepare food, but it might be the custom here that women were excluded from such tasks.

"Thanks," he said, "but I can manage. Besides, you still need to rest. How are you feeling?"

"Fine," she assured him, slightly flustered by his sudden scrutiny. He had raised his eyes and was looking directly at her. The dark velvet of his gaze drew her as the eddies of a whirlpool might. She felt as though she was falling from a great height, and had to wrench herself away with considerable effort.

"You're still very pale," he said.

She had noticed the contrasting shades of their skin earlier, but now she was struck even more by the fact. Compared to everything else surrounding her, it was only a small detail, yet it said so much about the differences between them. He lived beneath the sun, saw it rise each morning and set each night, felt its heat and was exposed to its rays. The thought of that both frightened and enticed her.

She sat down on the stool next to Billy. There was a small box on the counter. As she watched, Andrew leaned forward and pushed a button on it. "If you don't mind, I'd like to watch the news."

She kept silent, not wishing to reveal that she didn't understand what he meant. In the next moment, she forgot to worry about that. The box had sprung to life. A man's face appeared. His lips moved, and she heard his voice.

Only just managing to stifle a gasp of shock, she stared mesmerized at the box. Neither Andrew nor Billy seemed at all surprised by it, so she had to presume this was what it was supposed to do. With an effort, she concentrated on what the speaker was saying.

"Seals 14, Titans 7. And that's the sports, folks. Back in a moment with this evening's wrap-up."

The man disappeared, and a woman took his place. She was singing as she danced around a room that looked much like the one in which Marina was sitting. While she danced, she pushed a long stick with what looked like a sponge on its end.

"Dirt and dust go away
When you mop with Shine-All
Don't come back 'till another day
When you mop with Shine-All!"

Whatever she was doing, it seemed to be making her very happy. Marina was disappointed when the woman vanished and the man reappeared. He grinned at her, as though he was about to share a joke, and said, "And here's a little item from our What next? file. It seems some folks are pretty well convinced they've found evidence that the lost civilization of Atlantis actually existed. Not only that, but they say they've pinpointed its location and are going to launch a full-scale underwater excavation. I guess that just goes to prove that nothing's too crazy in this crazy world of ours."

"What's 'lantis?" Billy asked.

"It's a legend," his father explained, "about a place that existed a long time ago."

"What's a legend?"

"A story that's fun to believe in but isn't really true."

The little boy frowned, thinking that over. "If it's not true, how can they find it?"

Andrew shrugged and carried the salad over to the table. "I guess they think they can, or they wouldn't be trying. Go and wash your hands now."

Billy slipped off his stool and went to do as he was told. Marina stared at the box, where a young man and woman were gazing at each other rapturously while talking about going to some place called McDonald's. She felt very cold and her stomach was clenched. Unconsciously, she wrapped her arms around herself.

The box went blank. Andrew had flicked the button again. He looked at her and asked, "How do you like your steak?"

"My what?"

"Your steak." He gestured toward the platter of raw meat on the counter.

She stared at the steaks, wondering if he would believe her if she said she wasn't hungry. That happened to be the truth; her appetite had fled, and she wondered how she would be able to swallow a morsel of food. But rather than appear an ungrateful guest, she said, "I would like it cooked, please."

Andrew's eyes narrowed. He stared at her for a moment before shrugging his shoulders lightly. "Sure thing."

By the time Billy returned, the steaks were sizzling on a grill set into the counter. What appeared to be briquets of charcoal glowed beneath them. Marina was at a loss to understand why they didn't produce smoke. Seeing her puzzlement, Andrew said, "It's a Jennair."

That told her precisely nothing, but she pretended to understand and nodded. At any rate, the steaks were smelling better by the moment. She was feeling more at ease when they took their seats at the table. When the slab of cooked meat was placed on the plate before her, accompanied by finger-length pieces of what she believed to be a fried vegetable, she gathered her courage and wondered where to begin.

Andrew inadvertently helped her by cutting up Billy's meat for him. Meanwhile, the little boy poured a red sauce on top of the vegetable and proceeded to eat with his fingers. Marina bravely followed suit, finding that the sauce was spicy and not at all unpleasant, and that the vegetable, while tasting unlike anything she had ever encountered before, was perfectly tolerable.

The steak wasn't bad, either. She had some trouble with the knife and fork, but thought she managed them without calling any undue attention to herself. The sensation of chewing meat was odd; it required much more effort than fish. But to her great relief, her stomach did not recoil when she swallowed. She thought perhaps the dry, charcoal taste helped. For a moment after swallowing that first bite, she held her breath. Though she prided herself on her common sense, she was not so completely free of superstition that she could blithely ignore the taboo against eating meat. Not until she was convinced that no retribution would be forthcoming did she manage to relax and enjoy the rest of the meal.

The salad with its medley of vegetables, most of which were foreign to her, also had a sauce on it. Here at least she recognized flavors—the sweetness of oil,

the tang of vinegar, the bite of garlic. The wine Andrew
poured for her and himself was dryer than what she
was accustomed to, but very pleasant. The cheese and
fruit that followed were almost a touch of home; she
quelled a spurt of homesickness as she bit into a grape
and felt the sweet juice trickle down her throat.

While they ate, they talked. Marina took the initia-
tive, sensing that if she didn't, Andrew would begin to
ask questions that she might not find easy to answer.
Besides, she told herself, it was her job to question.

"Have you lived in the Caribbean long?" she began.

"A couple of years. How about you?"

Disconcerted to have the question thrown back at her
so quickly, she answered automatically. "I was born
not far from here." Before he could ask exactly where,
she turned her attention to Billy. With a smile, she said,
"It's a lovely place for a child to grow up."

The little boy nodded enthusiastically. "Like it
here."

Marina had noticed the absence of a woman in the
house, other than the housekeeper Andrew had mentioned. She was curious about that, but couldn't think
of a polite way to ask what had happened to Billy's
mother. Andrew saved her the trouble of trying. Quietly, he said, "We came here several months after my
wife died. Billy was a year old then. I was looking for
someplace peaceful where I could bring him up and
pursue my work. This fit the bill."

"What kind of work do you do?" Marina asked. She
was too perceptive to offer him routine condolences for
a tragedy that had clearly wounded him deeply. From
the first moment she glimpsed him, she had felt the
sadness in him beneath layers of quiet strength and

acceptance. Now she understood the cause and her respect for him increased accordingly.

"I'm a theoretical physicist," he said. With a grin, he added, "That means I spend my time puttering around with numbers. I have an office next to the house and a computer that links me to the mainland, at least when I want it to."

Marina suspected that he did a good deal more than "puttering." She was no stranger to the demands of pure research, but what did surprise her was that he had apparently been left free to pursue his interests on his own terms. That was a luxury few were ever afforded where she came from.

"Are you associated with a university?" she asked, seeing the only explanation she could think of.

He shook his head. "I've got a research grant from the government." At that he broke off, and she sensed he would say nothing more. The reason he didn't feel at ease to talk about his work eluded her, but she accepted it and didn't attempt to probe further.

They finished the meal in silence. Andrew cleared the dishes, having politely turned down Marina's offer of help. She was feeling somewhat at a loss as to what to do when Billy took her by the hand and said, "Read me a story?"

She glanced at his father for permission. He looked a bit surprised, but had no objection. "Go ahead. There's a bunch of his books in the den. I'll join you when I'm done here."

Marina was deep into the story of "Peter and the Wolf," with sound effects provided by Billy, when Andrew came in. He paused at the door and looked at them for a moment before lowering himself into a leather armchair across from the couch where they sat.

Marina had an arm around Billy, and he had snuggled against her; together they were looking at the pictures in the book, which she explained in between reading the story.

Andrew's throat tightened. His son looked so eager to be close to Marina and so comforted by her presence. He told himself that a motherless child was likely to attach himself to any woman who treated him kindly, but deep inside he knew that wasn't the case. Not even Hildy, who had cared for Billy since they came to Angle Key, provoked such a look in him. Billy was eager for his father to marry again simply so he would be like the other children he knew. But he was not particularly eager to either give or receive love from anyone but Andrew himself. At least, not until now.

That Billy should develop so sudden an attachment to a woman his father knew virtually nothing about, who had arrived in their lives under—to say the least— unusual circumstances, and who would undoubtedly shortly be leaving them, troubled Andrew deeply. He felt a sudden flash of resentment at Marina, which prompted him to ask, "Have you given any more thought to how you'll get home?"

As a matter of fact, she had, but that was the last thing she wanted to talk about just then. Particularly not when it interrupted the pleasant time she had been having with Billy. Nonetheless, she said quietly, "Yes, I have. You have been generous to extend your hospitality to me, but I will not intrude on it much longer."

Andrew flushed slightly. She had managed to make him feel churlish, as though he were in a hurry to see the back of her. Nothing could be farther from the truth. He had never encountered so enticing a woman, one who with very little effort could make him forget even the rudiments of common sense. Dressed as she was, in his clothes, her hair still somewhat tangled and her face as nature had made it, she should have had no more than a certain gamine prettiness. But the intelligence that shone from her sea-green eyes, the innate dignity with which she carried herself and the tenderness she exhibited whenever she looked at Billy endowed her with a transcendent beauty.

Andrew became aware that he was staring at her with an intensity that could be considered rude. With an effort, he wrenched his gaze away. "Go on with the story. I'm sorry I interrupted."

Marina complied, and he found himself listening to the soft rise and fall of her voice as he might to the rhythms of the sea. It had much the same effect on him. The tension eased from his long body. The problems he was having with his work, which were never far from his mind, suddenly seemed less important. His ever-present concerns about Billy and whether or not he was doing right by him dissipated. Without his being aware of it, his breathing became more regular, and his eyes closed. The long night he had spent keeping vigil over Marina had taken its toll. He slipped away into dreamless sleep.

When he awoke, it was dark. Someone had switched the light off. He sat up abruptly, only to discover that he had been covered with the afghan. It slipped to the floor as he got to his feet and looked around hurriedly.

There was no sign of Billy. Not that there should have been, since it was well past his bedtime. But Andrew had never before entrusted his son to anyone without being aware of what he was doing and being very careful about it. The idea that he had fallen asleep, leaving Billy alone with a woman he barely knew, shocked him. It wasn't that he really thought anything untoward might have happened, only that he needed to be absolutely sure it hadn't.

He covered the short distance down the hall to Billy's room with quick strides. At the door, he paused. There was no sound from within. Cautiously, he cracked open the door and peered inside. The lamb night-light had been turned on, and by its glow he could see clearly. Billy lay on his bed on his side. He was in his favorite Mickey Mouse pajamas, his blanket beside him. He looked utterly content and at peace.

With a sigh of relief, Andrew shut the door and went farther down the hall to the guest room. If Marina was still awake, he meant to thank her. But the door to the guest room was ajar, and there was no sign of anyone inside. Curious as to where she might be, he strolled through the house looking for her, only to find it empty.

He was standing in the kitchen, thoroughly perplexed, when he happened to glance out the window and saw her walking down the path toward the beach. The path curved, and he caught a glimpse of her profile. She looked preoccupied, even distant, as though there was something very much on her mind.

Knowing that she was unacquainted with the path and had no way of knowing how steep and rough it was, Andrew went after her. If she wanted to wander around in the dark, it was fine with him, but he certainly couldn't have her getting hurt in the process. Besides, though he was reluctant to admit it, he was becoming more curious about her by the moment. She might not be willing to tell him where she was going, or why, but he still intended to find out.

Chapter 3

Marina was too absorbed in her thoughts to be aware that she was no longer alone. She had been drawn outside by the sheer glory of the sky. Wherever she looked, a thousand stars gleamed.

The bright swath of the Milky Way could be clearly seen. She could make out the Mother Bear with her cub, Orion the Hunter stalking his prey, and the twins, Castor and Pollux, linked forever in the heavens. There was no moon, which she regretted, for she would have liked to have seen that, but what was on view was more than enough, more than she could ever have imagined from the brief glimpses of the sky she'd had before. She had thought the day was beautiful, but the night more than rivaled it.

Only with difficulty did she remember that she had a purpose in leaving the house other than simply to admire the view. The path from the house led down to the beach. She took it quickly, the way smoothed by a memory that was not her own. Billy knew the path well; now so did she. At the bottom, she walked across the expanse of sand, which was still warm from the vanished sun. Standing at the water's edge, she felt the tiny waves wash against her sandals and toes. An ineffable sense of yearning filled her.

This world, with all its conflict and danger, was even more beautiful than she had suspected. Not only was it lovely in itself, but it harbored such people as Andrew and Billy, both of whom she was loath to leave. The child held her out of simple need and because she had always responded to the young. The man was a different matter. She didn't care to examine too closely why he stirred her as he did, but she knew that even after such a short acquaintance, parting from him was going to be extremely difficult.

But part she must. Like it or not, she had to return to where she belonged, both to face the consequences of what she had done and to try to convince others that it had been worthwhile. She did not underestimate the enormity of that task. Her request for permission to make the journey had been vehemently denied. That she had done so anyway was bound to have aroused considerable ire.

How much she did not know, until she let her mind stretch forward to brush against the mind she knew would be searching for her.

"Marina!" Her brother spoke with great relief, and equal urgency. *"Where are you? It's been hours since the last contact. I thought something might have happened."*

"I'm fine, Theseus," she assured him quickly, regretful of the worry she had caused. Of all her family, he was closest to her. In age they were barely a year

apart. They looked enough alike to often be mistaken for twins. From childhood, they had been natural allies and coconspirators in the mischief children get into. She was still, she thought wryly, involving him in her mischief.

"Everything's all right," she said, "except that I lost the pod. There was a storm and—"

"Never mind about that," Theseus broke in. "Are you hurt?"

"No, I told you, I'm fine. I was rescued by a man and a boy. They've taken good care of me." Try though she did to hide it, she knew there was something in her thoughts that alerted Theseus to what she was not saying. She sensed that he wanted to question her about it, but didn't because of even more pressing concerns.

"There's trouble here," he said. "Your departure was noticed sooner than we had expected. It set off quite an outcry. The council is split in two about what sort of reception you should get when you return. Half are in favor of treating you like a heroine, but the other half are just as eager to see you slapped in jail."

"And Orestes," she asked softly. "What does he think?"

Theseus snorted with displeasure. She could feel his sarcasm and derision across all the miles separating them. "Our good uncle, the revered high councillor, says you're an example of everything that's wrong with our generation. He claims you must be punished in order to prevent others from following in your footsteps. If he has his way, you'll be denied even the right to tell what you've seen and learned."

"But that's terrible," Marina exclaimed. "We can't continue to go on pretending that the Outer World *doesn't exist. Far from going away, it's coming ever closer to us. Why only this evening, I heard—''*

She stopped, abruptly aware of a sound behind her. Turning, she saw nothing for a moment. Only when Andrew moved again did he stand out enough from the surrounding darkness for her to perceive him.

''Are you all right?'' he asked softly. ''You've been standing there so still and quiet, I didn't want to break into your thoughts, but it is late, and you might be better off in bed.''

Marina didn't answer at once. She was struck by how different he looked from the last time she had seen him. Asleep in the chair, he had appeared somehow younger and less formidable. Awake, that impression was banished. He radiated virile strength that touched her like coils of fire and provoked an answering warmth. It was difficult, given that, to be conscious of anything other than the long-drawn-out note of desire reverberating between them, as if from the tightly pulled string of a lyre echoing in Hall.

''Marina…'' It was Theseus calling her, rightly sensing that something had gone amiss, but unsure what it might be.

Deliberately, in a way she knew he wouldn't like but would understand, she shut down the contact between them. Her last words to him were a promise that she would be back in touch again soon. But in the meantime, Andrew demanded all her attention.

''Thank you for your concern,'' she said gravely. ''I couldn't sleep, so I thought I would get some fresh air.''

''The path is rough. You could have been hurt.''

''As you can see, I was not.''

He could hardly argue there, but neither could he

simply leave her. If he had followed his strongest impulses, he would have gone to her right then. But he sensed her wariness and, added to his own, it kept him at least at arm's length.

To distract himself, he said, "You took care of Billy. I appreciate that."

She glanced down at the ribbons of sea foam gleaming iridescently in the starlight. "It was my pleasure."

He took a step toward her and felt his bare feet sink farther into the warm sand. "Do you have much experience with children?"

"Some. I come from a large family."

"Sometimes I wish I did. I was an only child."

"There were times," she said with a rueful smile, "when I would have envied you."

"It was all right. My parents made sure I wasn't lonely. But tell me about your family. How many are there?"

"Six altogether. Myself, two other girls, and three boys. Several of them have married and had children, so I have nieces and nephews now. Then, of course, there are the brothers and sisters of my grandparents, whose children are my great-aunts and uncles. Both my parents had siblings, in addition, who also had children. I have perhaps two dozen cousins and, to date, not quite a dozen second cousins."

She would have continued, but Andrew held up a hand, laughing. "Hold on. I'm getting lost. This sounds like one of those incredibly extended families we hear about, almost like a clan."

Marina shot him a puzzled look that the darkness helped to obscure. That was exactly what her family was—a clan. She saw no reason to be surprised by it, but it occurred to her that customs might be very different among his people. "Your family is not close?"

"I guess not, compared to yours. I've got relatives in the States somewhere, but we haven't been in touch in years. Both my parents are dead, and I never knew any of my grandparents."

"How sad," she murmured, wondering what it must be like to live without the complex, sometimes frustrating but always reassuring clan ties that she had taken for granted since birth. No one she knew was in a remotely similar position; even those who might be unfortunate enough to lose their parents in childhood would immediately be taken up by a whole network of relatives. To allow a man or woman to fall out of touch with the family unit that was the foundation of society was unthinkable. One might as well try to raise a mighty tower on pillars of air and expect it to stand.

"This big family of yours," he said. "Is there some reason you don't want to get in touch with them?"

"Don't want to? But..." She stopped herself, realizing that from his point of view, that was the likeliest explanation for her unwillingness to call anyone for help. He had no way of knowing that she *had* called, though not in a fashion he could understand.

Dissembling did not come easy to her. She thought hurriedly, struggling to fabricate an excuse he would be inclined to believe. "Actually, I'm a bit embarrassed about the situation I'm in. But don't worry," she added quickly. "I can look after myself. I won't impose on you much longer. I'm planning to leave in the morning."

"And go where?" He hadn't meant to be as blunt as that, but the thought of her going off alone irked him. "You don't seem to know anyone around here who you could turn to, and, as I've already pointed out, you don't have any money or credit cards. So just how do you intend to manage?''

''I...I thought I'd get a job.'' For the spur of the moment, she didn't think that was bad. But Andrew apparently wasn't impressed.

''Doing what?'' he demanded. ''What kind of work do you expect to get without references? Besides, if you did manage to find a job, it wouldn't pay enough for you to live on. Since you say you come from this area, you must have some idea of how expensive everything is.''

In fact, she didn't, though she presumed that it was better to have money than not to. The obstacles he had raised concerned her. When she had set out on her voyage, she had expected to make landfall only very briefly, certainly not long enough to be faced with the problem of surviving there. Now she had to reconsider that.

The destruction of her craft had been bad enough, but she had assumed she would be rescued promptly. That could still be arranged, but if it was, she would be at a loss as to how to deal with her uncle and his determination to silence her. Despite the opposition of half the council, Orestes still had the power to prevail.

He could lock her away somewhere and make sure that no one outside a very limited circle ever learned what she had done. Not that she thought he would keep her incarcerated forever. He was far too clever to do anything that would invite his removal by other members of their family. Rather, he would simply make a deal, granting her freedom and forgiveness in return for her cooperation.

She would be faced with the choice of either remaining in prison and being silenced that way, or accepting release in exchange for a pledge that, once given, she would not be able to break. Moreover, if her family threatened to reveal what she had done in order to bring about her release, Orestes would simply point out that she had broken fundamental laws and that, should her transgressions become known publicly, he would have no choice but to punish her for them.

Her only hope was to remain away long enough for the opposition to her uncle to grow, at least to the point where he would have to allow her to return on her own terms. But to do that, she had to provide herself with the essentials for a life where everything was new and strange to her.

"I hadn't really thought," she said slowly, "of how difficult it would all be."

"I suppose you aren't accustomed to looking out for yourself." He didn't really expect her to deny it. As he watched her mull over what he had said, he thought he had figured out what it was about her that made her seem so different from both himself and the people he was used to.

He had decided that she probably came from a very wealthy family, which would explain the luxurious if unusual clothes he had found her in, her apparent lack of concern about such mundane realities as the destruction of her boat, and her refined manner, which he imagined was the result of some exclusive finishing school's best efforts. She had probably never in her life had to worry about such things as feeding herself and putting a roof over her head. In all likelihood she had no idea how difficult those tasks could be.

That she might soon find out troubled him. He was oddly stirred to protect and help her. "Are you sure," he asked in a last-ditch effort to make her see reason, "that you don't want to contact your family?"

"I'm sure," she said firmly. "I know it won't be easy, but I can look out for myself."

In a pig's eye! Andrew thought. She wouldn't have a chance of finding a job on Angle Key, where every opening was snapped up by someone anxious to live on the bucolic island. And if she went over to the bigger islands, she would confront an even tougher environment, where anything was likely to happen to her.

He hesitated a moment longer, then took a deep breath and said, "If you're serious about hanging around for a while, there is a job you might be interested in. It pays pretty well, and room and board go along with it."

"What kind of job is it?" Marina asked, eager for anything that might improve her situation. He had been sounding so grim that she had gotten genuinely worried, but now it seemed he had the solution ready at hand.

"Taking care of Billy." At her surprised look, he explained. "Hildy's going to be away for a while yet—her sister's sicker than she thought at first, and she can't leave her alone. I told her not to worry about it, but the fact is, her absence is causing me some problems. I've got a ton of work to get through, but I can't just leave Billy to his own devices. He needs pretty constant looking after, since he's at an age where he gets into everything. The two of you seem to have hit it off, so I was wondering if you'd be willing to lend me a hand. It could be the answer to both our difficulties."

"It sounds perfect," Marina said quickly. She could hardly believe her luck. Only now that it seemed she wouldn't have to, could she admit to herself how little she had been looking forward to striking out on her own. It wasn't that she wouldn't have been able to manage; she possessed skills Andrew knew nothing about. But this way was so much easier, besides which, it would permit her to remain with him awhile longer.

Mindful though she was of the potential dangers inherent in being near him, she told herself that she wouldn't do anything foolish. She would simply take the opportunity to learn more about his world and in the process to prepare herself for the confrontation she would face when she did get home.

"It's a lot of work," he cautioned, as though he thought she might be afraid of that.

Marina hid a smile, thinking of how rigorous her training had been from earliest childhood. Even if she had not been born into an aristocratic family that traced its lineage all the way back to the time of darkness, she would still have been expected to contribute and to fulfill her potential. That was how the people had survived and even prospered in an environment that would long ago have destroyed most others.

"I think I can handle it," she said softly. "As you pointed out, Billy and I get along fine."

Andrew couldn't resist a wry laugh. They had walked a short distance down the beach, and now, in silent accord, they turned toward the path that led to the house. As they did so, he said, "I'm afraid you've only seen Billy at his best, at least so far. Being raised without a mother has left some rough edges that need smoothing out."

He spoke matter-of-factly, neither asking for her sympathy nor expecting it. But she guessed what it cost him to admit that his son had been denied anything, even that which it was not in his father's power to give. He could not, after all, simply fall in love with the first available female who looked as though she would make a good mother. And without love, any second marriage he might have made would have done Billy no good at all.

"He's a wonderful little boy," she said. "I'm sure that, whatever those rough edges are, they don't amount to much."

"No," Andrew agreed. "He is a good kid. But he has a tendency to test people, as though he needs to discover whether or not they're going to let him down."

"That sounds like one of my nephews. He thought he was less intelligent and talented than his brothers and sisters, so he was constantly pushing his parents to see if they really loved him."

"What happened?" Andrew asked as they started up the path.

Marina laughed softly. "He drove them pretty well crazy until they pointed out to him that he was far more imaginative than anyone else in the family, at least when it came to getting into trouble. Not only that, but no one could beat him for sheer, bullheaded stubbornness." Except perhaps herself, but she saw no reason to mention that. "He was finally convinced that he had as many special attributes as anyone else, but that even without them, he would still have been loved simply for himself."

"It sounds," Andrew said as he reached out a hand to help her over a rough spot in the path, "as though you come from a very smart family. I wish I was that clever about being a parent."

She smiled in the darkness. "I imagine you do all right."

"I manage, but somehow I think it's going to be easier with you around." At least Billy would be looked after. But it would not, he knew, be easier for himself. Already he suspected that she was going to be a major-league distraction, one he would have to fight against not only in order to get his work done, but also to avoid an entanglement that could cost him far more than he could afford to give.

He had to remember that she was simply passing through, on her way back to a life far removed from his own. Had the feelings she inspired in him been at all casual, he wouldn't have cared. But he wanted her with an intensity that shocked him, and which brought with it an underlying tenderness that did not even have the reassuring ring of familiarity.

He had almost thought that, with the single exception of Billy, the need to love and be loved had been burned out of him. Now he was beginning to doubt that, and to fear the consequences of his own vulnerability.

He removed his hand from her arm and said brusquely, "Tomorrow we'll go buy you some clothes. Then you can get to work, and so can I."

He would bury himself in the fascinating, complex equations that demanded his attention. What free time he allowed himself, he would spend with Billy. While Marina was there, he would stay as far away from her as he possibly could. And when she left, he would forget her quickly.

Or so he told himself.

Chapter 4

Angle Key was a small backwater island among the American Virgins. Few tourists ever found their way to it. Those who did put up at small guest houses and found their amusements sunning on the white sand beaches or fishing the turquoise waters. There was no casino, none of the night life associated with the larger islands. It was said—perhaps boasted—that Angle Key went to bed with the sun and rose with it.

What the island did possess, in discreet profusion, were second, and in some cases third, homes belonging to the discerning wealthy. They nestled in the hills over the beach, hidden behind flowering bougainvillea and other tropical plants. Andrew's house was one of these; originally he had rented it, but a year before it had been put up for sale when the owner suffered reverses in the stock market. Andrew had bought it and become one of the relatively few year-round residents of the island. Slowly but steadily, he was beginning to feel at home there. Moreover, he was proud of Angle Key, and he didn't mind showing it off to Marina.

After breakfast the next morning, they went shopping. The island boasted a small harbor around which a cluster of stores had sprung up. They stopped first at the grocery to buy milk and other necessities. Andrew also placed an order for additional supplies, which had to be ferried in from one of the larger islands.

With Billy tagging along, they stopped next at the bookstore. It did a booming business, serving as it did customers with a natural disposition to quiet pursuits. Billy browsed through the children's section, while Andrew picked up several scientific volumes he had ordered.

Keeping one eye on Billy, Marina glanced at the bestseller rack. She was not at all surprised, though somewhat amused, to discover that the people of the Outer World had tastes similar to those of the Inner World, apparently enthralled by tales rampant with lust, greed and violence.

She replaced a book with a cover featuring a buxom young lady being carried off by a gentleman whose intentions were only too clear. Farther down the row of shelves she noticed a sign that said History and looked to see what that might include. She was staring in bemusement at one of the books she found there when Andrew joined her.

"What's that?" he asked, gesturing at the book.

She looked up with a start, having forgotten for a moment where she was and who she was with. Quickly she glanced toward Billy, who was still happily ensconced in the children's section. Andrew had taught him well about the proper behavior there. He was sitting cross-legged on the floor, leafing through the book he had picked out to buy.

Hastily, Marina replaced the book she had been reading intently, but not before Andrew saw the title.

"*History of Ancient Greece*. That interests you?"

"I just noticed it in passing. Did you get everything you wanted?"

He frowned, as though not quite believing her studied casualness. Again he glanced at the book. "We could get that, if you'd like."

She did, very much, but she didn't feel that she could reveal an interest that would only prompt further questions. Instead she said, "It's a little heavy for me, but thanks."

He shrugged and let it go, but she sensed that it was still on his mind as they paid for Billy's book and went next door. The clothing store was actually a small, exclusive boutique that catered to a clientele accustomed to the best. Andrew's theory about Marina's background seemed confirmed when she showed no surprise at the prices but instead simply glanced at the clothes with the air of a woman interested in fashion but hardly overwhelmed by it.

In fact, the prices didn't surprise her because she had no idea of how much anything cost. She lacked any sense of the value of money, so, to her, fifty dollars for a pair of shorts and a hundred for a skirt seemed perfectly reasonable. She was far more struck by the styles, which were quite different from what she was accustomed to, and the range of materials, some of which she had never seen before.

As she wandered about with Billy at her heels, she could hear Andrew explaining what was needed to the woman who ran the boutique. "Miss Lirularia was in

a boating accident and finds herself without a wardrobe. She needs the basics.''

"Of course, sir,'' the young, blond woman said with
a smile. She looked Marina up and down assessingly.
''Let's see…you're a size eight, I'd say.'' She began
pulling items off a rack. An assistant appeared to help
carry them into a dressing room.

"Go ahead,'' Andrew said when she glanced at him
questioningly. ''Billy and I will wait for you here.''

Without being quite aware of how it happened, she
found herself in the dressing room, standing in front of
a three-way mirror, with the blond woman extolling the
virtues of what she had selected. ''So versatile, these
linen pants,'' she said. ''You can dress them up with
a few gold chains and a nice belt. We have an excellent
choice of those.''

"I'm sure you do,'' Marina said, beginning to get a
grip on the situation. Not for nothing, after all, was she
the daughter of one of the Inner World's acknowledged
beauties and fashion setters. ''But I need clothes to
work in. I'll be looking after Mr. Paxton's little boy,
so some of these things simply won't be practical.''

As she spoke, she was going through the pile of
clothes, rejecting most of them. Silk shirts went, as did
the linen pants. Several pretty but flimsy dresses were
vetoed, along with a bathing suit so skimpy that Marina
had to wonder why anyone would bother wearing it.

Instead she chose a couple of cotton shirts, one pair
of shorts and a pair of slacks. From observation she
had determined that this was what most people on the
island wore. Since her goal was to blend in as unob-
trusively as possible, she thought it would be just as
well if she dressed like everyone else. Remembering

that Andrew had been disconcerted by her nudity, she also selected a simple, one-piece bathing suit.

"This will do," she said as the somewhat disgruntled woman was gathering up the rejects. "I'll just try them on to make sure they fit."

"You'll need a bra," the woman sniffed.

"A what?"

"A bra. I hope you don't mind my saying so, but you're a bit too large to be going around without one. Even in casual things, it ruins the line."

Marina wasn't at all sure what she was talking about, but she was willing enough to learn. With a shrug, she said, "I guess I'll need one of those, too."

The woman returned a few moments later and handed her the article of clothing in question. "I guessed at your size," she said. "34B, right?"

Marina glanced down at the contraption. It was white, trimmed with lace, and appeared to consist of two cup-shaped objects connected by a series of straps. It took her a moment to figure out its use, and when she did, she was tempted to laugh. Restraining herself with an effort, she assured the woman that her guess was probably correct, but if not, she would let her know.

Left alone, she stripped off her clothes and attempted to put on the bra. Her first attempt left her tangled up in the straps, one arm trapped against her chest and the other stuck up in the air. Having managed to extricate herself, she tried again, but with little more success. Only on the third try did she figure out that it was simpler to fasten the hooks behind her back before attempting to slip her arms through the shoulder straps.

When the bra was finally in place, she looked at herself in the mirror and tried to decide if it had been worth all that effort. She didn't really think so, though she had to admit that it was comfortable enough. More so than the breast bands the women she knew wore, and which she occasionally donned when fashion absolutely required it.

The clothes she had approved all fit. Wearing one of the shirts and the pair of slacks, she rejoined Andrew and Billy. The little boy immediately assured her that she looked very nice, but his father merely glanced at her and frowned.

"There are a few other things you'll need," he said, gesturing to a small pile in front of him.

Marina saw that it consisted of underpants in a range of soft colors, and a couple of nightgowns suitable to the balmy weather. The blond woman was doing her best to conceal a smirk, the source of which Marina did not have to wonder at. She made a mental note that the people of the Outer World were apparently not as comfortable with intimacy as she was accustomed to being.

"Thank you for all this," she said to Andrew as they left the boutique. "Of course, I will reimburse you." She had insisted on taking charge of the sales slip that gave the total of his expenditures, a figure she was beginning to suspect was rather high.

"Don't worry about it," Andrew said.

Marina let the matter rest, though she had made up her mind that he would be repaid whether he wanted to be or not. Where she came from, a man gave gifts to a woman, and she to him, as a declaration of intent. Moreover, she suspected that the same was true among his people. However much she was drawn to Andrew, they were hardly in that position. To pretend otherwise would only make an already difficult situation worse.

Billy skipped on ahead of them as they strolled away from the small cluster of shops toward a café on a pier jutting out over the water. "I thought we'd have lunch," Andrew said, "before heading home."

That was fine with Marina. She realized that she'd be taking on most of the cooking and felt certain that with a little luck she'd be able to cope, but she didn't mind a slight reprieve. Particularly since the café specialized in seafood. The variety was much slimmer than it would have been at home, but she was able to enjoy a meal more to her taste than anything she had had in the past couple of days.

If Andrew noticed her improved appetite, he didn't comment. When they were finished, they strolled around the harbor, where Marina found the different kinds of boats of great interest. It was midafternoon when they returned to the house. Billy had fallen asleep in the car. His father lifted him out and carried him to his room, where he put him down for a nap.

"I'll be in my office," he told Marina when he came back. "If you need anything, just holler."

She assured him that she could manage and firmly stilled the faint quiver of disappointment she felt at his departure.

Left to her own devices, she resolved to familiarize herself with the kitchen. Most of it was strange to her, but with a combination of intelligence and imagination, she was able to figure out how things worked. What astonished her most was not the strange foods she encountered or the array of cooking utensils she had to stretch her mind to identify, but the prodigious waste of energy. Most food apparently had to be cooked, which meant energy had to be used. As if that weren't bad enough, a great deal of the food was stored in a very large, cold box that, not content with keeping things chilled, also insisted on making ice.

She shook her head as she took note of the many lights recessed into the ceiling of the kitchen and remembered how many other lights there were throughout the house. Nowhere did she see the luminescent creatures that provided most of the illumination at home.

Considering the possibility that these objects might somehow be alive, she studied the switches, turning them on and off a few times, and even went so far as to get up on a stepladder to take a close look at one of the glass orbs from which the light emanated. All this led her to conclude that no life was involved, and that the principal energy was electrical.

She was no stranger to that, nor to the difficulties in its creation. Did the people of the Outer World possess such mastery over electricity that they could afford to be so spendthrift with it? If they had achieved that much, why hadn't they discovered the better forms of energy on which her own people relied? She wished there was some way she could ask Andrew.

After taking out the chicken he had suggested they have for dinner, she sprinkled it with a few herbs that reminded her of home and placed it in the oven. She then set the table, remembering how he had done it the evening before. When she was finished she sat down to study the paper, which had been delivered earlier in the day along with the mail.

It was, so far as she could make out, a paper from a city on the mainland, far from the islands. But it also carried news of the world, particularly on its first page. There she found an article about an accident in a nuclear power plant that left her more bewildered than enlightened; a review of a government scandal that seemed to involve money being provided to rebels in another country; and an interview with a man who was running for president, whatever that might be.

On the inside pages she discovered ads for women's clothes, which fascinated her, a review of a movie that, as far as she could figure out, seemed to be similar to a play, and something called a crossword puzzle, which quickly showed her how far she was from fluency in the language.

Far in the back, toward the bottom of a page, she came across a story that made her sit up abruptly.

Scientist Announces Discovery of Remains of Atlantis.

Renowned scientist and inventor, Tristan Ward, disclosed yesterday in a press conference that his *Questor* exploration team had discovered archaeological remains he identifies as belonging to the lost civilization of Atlantis, believed by many to be mythical. Professor Ward, who declined to reveal the location of the find beyond saying that it was in the Caribbean, said that the discovery was the result of two years' work. An artifact discovered during the first year's exploration bore writing identified as early Minoan by Professor Ward's linguist wife, Dr. Cassia Ward. In translation, the writing made a direct reference to Atlantis.

Since then Dr. Ward and his team have uncovered additional ruins at another site that appear to date from about 2000 B.C. and to have been destroyed by an earthquake or tidal wave.

No explanation for the presence of Greek artifacts in the Caribbean has been forthcoming from other scientists, but Dr. Ward acknowledged that his discoveries would be questioned and that agreement as to their nature would not come without further research and study. He indicated that he intends to continue his investigations.

Marina put the paper down slowly. It was worse than she had thought. Since word had first come that a section of the outlying territories, one long ago abandoned by the people of the Inner World, had drawn the attention of the Outworlders, there had been much concern about what they would find. People like her Uncle Orestes insisted that they would go off empty-handed, as so many other searchers had before them. But apparently he had been wrong. This Tristan Ward did not sound like someone who would give up easily, especially not now that his interest had been whetted.

For centuries, since the rediscovery of the Outer World, the controversy had raged. Some favored reestablishing contact; others insisted that would only pollute and weaken their perfect society. Marina understood both points of view, but, all things considered, she believed it was unrealistic to pretend the Outer World did not exist. It did, and sooner or later its energetic, curious, determined people would find what had remained hidden from them for so long.

She had spoken out to that effect in council and had been rewarded by a sharp set-down from her uncle. Lacking his support, and confronted by weak councillors who did not dare defy him regardless of their private beliefs, she had made the decision to take matters into her own hands.

Hence her secret voyage outside, where she had intended to remain only long enough to make the point that there was nothing intrinsically harmful there. On the contrary, whether the council liked it or not, the people of both worlds were one and the same. Four thousand years of separation had not changed that fundamental fact. Marina believed to the bottom of her heart that they belonged together.

Her brow knitted in worry, she folded the paper and put it aside. She would have to contact Theseus again soon. But, in the meantime, she had to keep her mind on her duties. Andrew had trusted her with a job to do; honor demanded that she fulfill that trust, no matter what her private concerns.

She looked in on Billy and found him still peacefully asleep. That gave her a chance to put in the laundry. She thought she was getting rather good at figuring out all the strange machines, but revised that when she put too much soap powder in the first time and had to re-wash the load.

By then Billy had awakened. She gave him a glass of milk and a cookie. After doing away with both, he suggested they go out to play.

"I'll show you my best places," he offered. "Even the secret ones."

She agreed, after making sure that the chicken wasn't done yet. Billy's hand in hers, they wandered around the garden and a short distance beyond. Marina admired the wildflowers he pointed out, the birds' nests high in the palms and those hidden in the ground cover, and the place where a colony of crabs had dug their burrows.

"They come out in the evening," he said. "You can see them then. They're called hermit crabs, and they live in other animals' shells."

Marina was quite familiar with the species, as she was with any number of others. Seeing Billy's interest, she began to tell him stories about other kinds of sea life: of the great white whales, who had a rich language in which they sang when they were in love; of the porpoises and dolphins, whose minds were as keen as any man's, and who had created a complex culture all their own; and of the hidden places in the ocean floor, where all manner of wonders occurred. Of these last, she was careful not to say too much, though she couldn't resist mentioning that there were marvels beneath the waves that few would ever guess at.

The sun was fading in the west when they returned to the house. Andrew watched them coming. After several less-than-fruitful hours spent trying to work, he had given up the effort. Perhaps tomorrow would be better. In the meantime, he had decided to see how Marina was doing.

Apparently very well, if the way Billy looked at her was anything to go by. The woman and child walking hand in hand in the waning light might have been a portrait of maternal devotion and the love it inspired. Marina was all slender beauty and grace, her midnight black hair falling over one shoulder as she gazed down at the boy. Billy said something, and she laughed. The sound reached Andrew through the still air. He let it sink into him and touch some hidden wellspring that had, for too long, been dry.

He crossed the flagstone patio toward them. They saw him coming and waited, as though they were both a bit uncertain about how he would respond to the relationship springing up between them. He let them know by reaching down for Billy and swinging him toward the sky. The little boy squealed with pleasure; it was his favorite game.

"More, Daddy," he yelled, and Andrew complied. His arms were strong, the muscles well-defined beneath the thin cotton shirt he wore. Marina watched his biceps clench and unclench as he lifted the child again and again, until Billy was breathless with laughter and willing to stop. He let himself be put down and scampered off toward the house.

"Such energy," Marina said with a rueful smile. Her eyes met Andrew's in a moment of perfect understanding. "It must have been very difficult for you."

He knew what she referred to and silently thanked her for having the tact not to mention Elizabeth's death directly. That was for him to do. "There were times," he said quietly as they continued to walk toward the house, "when I didn't think I would survive it. Perhaps I wouldn't have, if Billy hadn't needed me so much."

"You must have loved her a great deal."

"I did," he agreed promptly. "But...since she died...there are things I've realized...." He had never talked about them with anyone, and he didn't understand why he was tempted to do so now. He only knew that Marina's presence soothed him and gave him the courage to look at places in his soul that had been too painful for close scrutiny.

"Elizabeth was an only child, like myself. I think we both believed that gave us some special understanding of each other that would be a good beginning for a marriage. We didn't realize that we had virtually nothing else in common. She came from a very wealthy family; mine was strictly working class. I was the first kid to go to college, much less go further. I grew up thinking that if you wanted something, you worked for it. Elizabeth's expectations were very different.''

"She thought the world was an easier place than you knew it to be?"

"Yes, I suppose that was it. At any rate, she couldn't understand why I was so absorbed by my work. I went into physics in the beginning simply because I was good at it, and I knew I could use it to earn a decent living. But, before very long, I was fascinated. The further I went, the more the fascination grew. In the end, Elizabeth accused me of caring more about my work than I did about her.''

"Was that true?"

He looked at her sharply. "You don't pull any punches, do you? Most people would have assured me it couldn't possibly have been."

"Why not? You're describing a wife whom I'm sure was very lovely in many respects, but who was also essentially still a child. It wouldn't be strange at all for you to take your work more seriously than you did her.''

"Elizabeth disagreed," he said without bitterness. "We became trapped in a vicious cycle. The more she demanded my attention, the more I gave it to my work instead, and the more insecure she became. We were on a downhill slide to nowhere when she announced that she was pregnant.''

"How did you feel about it?"

"Angry, at first. We hadn't talked about it, and I thought she'd only gone ahead on her own to keep me in the marriage. Afterward, of course, I was ashamed of that.''

"After she died?"

He nodded. "Billy was six months old. She left him

at home with me, something she'd taken to doing frequently, and went out to have lunch with a girlfriend. It turned out to be a pretty liquid lunch. On the way home, she drove off the side of a cliff."

Marina sucked in her breath sharply. She had suspected all along that there was something like that buried beneath the layers of his self-control, but hearing it revealed so starkly gave her a cold chill. No wonder he had come to Angle Key seeking peace.

"You blame yourself," she said, not questioning what was so clearly fact to her.

"How could I do otherwise? She needed understanding and patience; I gave her neither."

"And she gave you a child. No wonder you feel the equation doesn't balance."

He gave her another of those sharp looks she was becoming accustomed to. "I suppose I do tend to think of the world in those terms," he said.

"It's how your mind is shaped. Who could blame you?"

He laughed, a little disconcerted. "You'd be surprised. I have a hard time accepting it myself. But tell me, so long as we're discussing minds and their shaping, how did you come to be so perceptive?"

She wanted to tell him of the birth gift and the rites that shaped it, of the hours of meditation fading into the days and weeks necessary to bring the gift to full fruition, of the pain she sometimes suffered even now when it became too sharp to bear. But she could say none of that, not because he wouldn't understand, but because he might.

"I am the youngest of six children," she said instead, "born to a father and mother who were frequently at war with one another. Under such circumstances, one learns to see and hear very clearly.''

''What happened to your parents?''

''My father died.'' She didn't offer to tell him how, though she would have liked to. For all his faults, her father had died courageously, supporting one of the immense buttresses that kept out the sea. He had won enough time for the engineers to come with their emergency pumps, but they hadn't been fast enough to keep the life from fleeing from his crushed body.

''And your mother?'' Andrew prompted gently.

''She married again, a distant kinsman who would have taken us into his house, but by then we were all old enough to look after ourselves.''

''I think,'' Andrew said, ''that I've figured out where you come from.''

Marina felt what little color there was in her face drain away. ''I've made no secret of it. I told you, I'm from around here.''

''Actually, you said another group of islands, but you didn't specify which. Anyway, wherever you were born, your accent is Greek.'' He looked rather proud of his discovery and didn't hesitate to add, ''That must be why you're interested in Greek history.''

''Do I really sound Greek?''

''A little. I spent several summers there, mostly traveling around the islands. To be precise, you sound like the people I met on Crete.''

''How interesting.''

''It's a fascinating place. Ever been there?''

''No,'' she said, ''though I've always wanted to go.''

''You'd fit right in. Now, will you tell me if my guess is right?''

She hesitated a moment, then nodded. "You must have a very good ear. It's true that my forebears came from Crete."

"How did they end up here in the Caribbean?"

"That," she said with a faint smile, "is a long story." And one she had absolutely no intention of telling him.

Chapter 5

While they were walking to the house, Billy came across an injured bird, one of the small brown doves that frequented the islands in winter. When the warmer weather came they migrated north, where their distinctive cooing could be heard as far as New England.

But the one Billy found wouldn't be going anywhere unless his broken wing was treated. The boy came to them with the bird cupped in his hands. His small face was solemn as he held them up. "Look."

Marina reached out a finger and stroked the bird's head with the lightest of touches. She felt its pain and its fear. Gently, under her breath, she crooned to it. After a moment its eyes closed and it grew perceptibly more relaxed in the hands of its small rescuer.

"Let's take it inside," she said. "I saw some small sticks in your room that will make a good splint."

Billy nodded, gave the bird to her and ran on ahead.

He was waiting for them when she and Andrew arrived.

"They're for building with," he said, handing her the sticks, "so they've never been in a popsicle. They're clean."

"That's what we need," Marina said, her attention on the bird. She took it into the kitchen and laid it gently on the table. It made a feeble effort to escape, all it was capable of, but settled down when she took up the crooning again.

Billy watched, as did his father, while she deftly set the wing, then persuaded the bird to take a small amount of sugar water. She put it to rest in a shoe box and only then remembered the chicken.

Andrew beat her in the dash to the oven, pulled it out without mittens on and dropped it quickly, pan and all, onto the counter. "There's no harm done," he assured her when she insisted on examining his hands. They were reddened, but there was no sign of blisters.

"You were lucky," she said. "We could have managed without the chicken."

"I didn't want your first meal for us to be ruined."

Neither did she; at home it would have been considered very bad luck. Even in such modern times, a bride who spoiled the first meal she prepared for her husband cast a few drops of water on the cook fire to placate the spirits. But then, Andrew wasn't her husband, and she was foolish to be thinking that way.

As it turned out, the chicken was fine. Billy ate his fill and went off to bed after entrusting the still-sleeping bird to Marina. Andrew insisted on helping with the dishes. She couldn't help but wish that he would meet some of the men she knew who thought such things beneath them.

Afterward they sat in the den watching television. She was reminded of the evenings in the Hall spent listening to the bard, although honesty compelled her to admit that the quality was far higher there. Still, she enjoyed a program about people working in a law firm, amused to discover that the rendering of justice seemed to be equally confused everywhere.

When the program was over, the news came on. There was no mention of the Wards and their search for Atlantis. Marina did not presume that meant anything; on the contrary, her experience had taught her that news of any importance was often kept hidden.

"It's getting late," Andrew said when they had heard the last of the sports and been assured that the next day's weather would be fair. "I think I'll turn in."

She was unfamiliar with that expression, but discerned its meaning easily enough. It was late, and she was tired. With a full day of looking after Billy ahead of her, she wanted to be at her best.

"I will, too," she said, rising from the couch where they had been sitting side by side, though not close enough to touch. "Thank you for everything you did today."

"You don't have to thank me," he said, standing also. "I was glad to do it. Besides," he reminded her with a slightly crooked smile, "you've insisted you'll pay me back."

"A debt must always be paid," she replied gravely. In standing, they had moved closer together, enough for her to be vividly aware of his size and strength. He moved with the grace of an athlete. She thought he would do well in the Games. The image of him naked, his skin oiled, poised on the playing field to hurl a discus or a javelin, made her flush.

"What are you thinking about?" he asked.

"Nothing."

His smile deepened, becoming very male. "Not true. You're thinking about the same thing I am."

"Thoughts are private."

"And a debt is always to be repaid. It sounds as though you were brought up on a combination of Ben Franklin and Socrates."

"Who are they?" The words were out before she could stop them.

His dark brown eyes widened slightly in the instant before his lids dropped to hide his surprise. "You're kidding," he said.

"Of course." She gave him a smile she knew to be both too quick and too bright, revealing her nervousness.

"Ben Franklin was one of the all-time great ball players, right?"

She nodded quickly. "The greatest."

"And Socrates, you can't find a better actor than him. Did you see his latest movie?"

"Uh...no, I missed that, but you're right, he's the best."

"Wouldn't be surprised if he cops an Oscar."

"Right," she said, edging toward the door. "Well, I think I'll be going to bed."

"You do that." He had slid his hands into the pockets of his slacks, but she could see that his fists were clenched. It occurred to her that she had said something wrong. She had no idea what to do about that, so retreat seemed the best strategy.

"Good night," she murmured as she left the den, closing the door softly behind her.

* * *

Andrew continued to stare at the spot where she had been for several moments before he cursed under his breath and jerked himself away. What a hell of a situation! He, who had always mocked Longfellow for his concerns about security, was suddenly face-to-face with the possibility that he had brought a major security breach right into his own home. Not only that, he had allowed himself to be intensely drawn to her.

Before he could pursue that line of thought any further, he went over to the small built-in bar, helped himself to two fingers of Scotch and drank them down neat. The liquor burned his throat, but he barely noticed. He stared unseeingly into the empty glass before absently putting it aside and beginning to pace.

As always, he first sought to approach the problem logically. Although no one had ever said so straight out, he had always presumed that the concerns about keeping his work secret centered around the fear that the Russians might try to steal it. After all, it was inevitably the Russians that people like Longfellow worried about, wasn't it? That was their job; he supposed somebody had to do it, but he had always thought it a singularly narrow approach, not allowing for all sorts of other interesting permutations and possibilities.

That didn't matter right now. What counted was that, try as he did, he couldn't imagine the Russians—or, for that matter, anyone else—sending out an agent as abysmally prepared as Marina seemed to be. That she didn't know who Ben Franklin was just might be written off to ignorance of American history; there were undoubtedly millions of equally ill-informed people, including more than a few Americans themselves. But Socrates? That was a different matter altogether, especially given her admission of a Greek heritage and her interest in Greek history.

How could she not know who Socrates was?

Briefly, he considered the possibility that she hadn't heard him correctly. He dismissed that, knowing that he was grasping at straws. Reluctantly, but with the strength of will that characterized everything he did, he forced himself to run down the list of anomalies he had noticed about her.

There were the clothes he'd found her in, for one. Again, they helped to rule out the agent idea, but they also required an explanation that she was clearly in no hurry to give. Then there was her refusal to tell him exactly where she had come from, her insistence that she couldn't contact her family, her apparent unconcern that anyone would be looking for her. No matter how hard he tried, he couldn't begin to make sense of it.

Balanced against all that were her gentleness and sensitivity, the beauty that he sensed was as much spiritual as it was physical. He thought of how good she was with Billy, and of how she had cared for the injured dove. He remembered how he had felt driven to confide in her about Elizabeth, and how sensibly she had responded.

He stopped pacing and sat down, staring at the phone and wondering if he should call Longfellow. But what would he say? If he so much as hinted that he had security concerns he'd be engulfed in protection before he could turn around. Yet his fundamental sense of responsibility wouldn't allow him to brush aside the questions Marina raised, but instead forced him to try to discover the truth before it might be too late for all of them.

The only way he could do that was to stay close by

her, keeping an eye out for anything that might reveal who and what she was. Which, now that he thought about it, wouldn't exactly be a hardship.

His mouth was set in a taut line, and his eyes gleamed with something that looked very much like anticipation when he flicked the den light off and went to bed himself.

Marina spent a restless night. After leaving Andrew, she went back over their conversation and decided that he had tricked her. The people he had referred to must have been the type anyone would know about.

She lay awake for a long time, staring at the ceiling and wondering what to do. She could leave, of course, but that would involve her in all the problems she had already considered. She could try to pretend she'd only been kidding, but it was unlikely that she could carry that off. For a while she thought about making up some story about her background that would explain her ignorance. If it hadn't been for the duplicity that plan required, she might have pursued it further.

She fell asleep at last, aware that Theseus was calling her, but unwilling to answer for fear of betraying more than she wanted her brother to know.

The next day she rose early, when the eastern sky was only beginning to turn light. No one else was stirring. She made coffee, as she had seen Andrew doing, and took a cup herself, having quickly developed a taste for it. Seated on the low stone wall that ran around the edge of the patio, she looked out over the dark water and watched the last pale stars flicker out.

So much space. Oddly, it didn't trouble her. At home, those who thought at all about the Outer World theorized that to go there might bring madness. They said that to stand beneath an unfettered sky and look directly up toward heaven would, after so many generations without such things, unhinge the mind. She had thought that nonsense, but a small fear had still followed her on her journey. It was banished now as she arched her neck to take out the night's kinks and smiled at the rising sun.

She was fixing breakfast for Billy when Andrew stuck his head in to say he wouldn't be joining them. "I want to make an early start," he explained.

"If you like," she offered, "I'll bring you a tray."

"Thanks, but that won't be necessary." He grabbed a cup of coffee, gave Billy a smile and a pat, and departed, having hardly glanced at Marina.

Again she found herself having to stifle a quiver of disappointment. At least he hadn't taken up where they had left off the night before. Perhaps she hadn't slipped up, after all. Feeling a shade more confident, she cleaned up after Billy, then persuaded him to let her give him a bath.

"What would you like to do this morning?" she asked as he splashed around in the tub amid a flotilla of floating toys.

"Go to the beach?" he suggested, catching hold of a transparent ball and twirling it around so that music played as brightly painted carousel horses revolved.

The aftereffects of the storm had died away during the night. Marina saw no reason why it wouldn't be safe. Accordingly, she helped Billy dress in a pair of trunks and a cover-up, then left him briefly while she put on the one-piece bathing suit Andrew had bought for her.

The door to his office was closed when they were

ready to leave. Rather than disturb him, she left a note
on the refrigerator telling him where they had gone.

Billy ran on ahead, though he was careful to obey
her injunction not to go too far ahead. The beach was
empty when they reached it. Marina spread the blanket
she had brought, anchoring it with small rocks Billy
found. That done, he wanted to go swimming immediately, but she shook her head.

"Let's wait until your breakfast has had a chance to
settle. How about a walk in the meantime? We can look
for shells."

He agreed readily enough, and they set out, leaving
their towels and snorkeling gear—including the set
Billy had found for her—on the blanket. Their pace
was slow as they diligently searched the sand at the
water's edge for whatever treasures it might yield.

"Look," Billy said, pointing excitedly. "A triton
shell. It's not even broken." He held it up to her, proud
of his discovery.

Marina took it, turning it in her hand, admiring the
pale yellow shell with its knobby spirals and opening
bright with golden opalescence. "It's beautiful," she
said, struck by the fact that Billy had called it by the
same name she would have. It would be a good idea
to collect more such instances before she returned
home. They would be useful in helping her convince
people that the inhabitants of the Outer World were not
complete aliens. They shared a common culture, however far in the past, that should help them achieve some
understanding of one another.

Her mind was still on that as she and Billy continued
to wander down the beach. They went as far as they
could, finding several more interesting shells along the
way, until they were stopped by an outcropping of

rocks jutting from the hillside into the water. Marina could have scrambled over them, but she didn't think it was a good idea to let Billy try. He made only a token protest, leading her to conclude that he was accustomed to going no farther.

Back at the blanket, they spread the shells out and admired them. The sun had climbed high in the sky, and Marina was beginning to feel uncomfortably warm. "How about that swim now?" she suggested.

With their snorkeling masks in place and their flippers in their hands, they returned to the water. "How about showing me what a good swimmer you are?" she asked, wanting to be sure of his skill before they started out.

She, who had swum before she could walk, was quickly impressed. Billy didn't have quite the skill that a child his age would have had at home, but he was very good. Reassured that he wouldn't run into trouble if they ventured into deep water, she put on her flippers and joined him.

For perhaps half an hour they cavorted in the water. Billy knew the location of a coral reef, which they dove to. They swam through a rainbow of parrot fish, paused to admire the iridescent beauty of an angelfish, and played tag with a somber but tolerant grouper before finally returning to the beach.

"That was fun," Billy declared as he flopped on the blanket. "Hildy isn't a good swimmer, and Daddy has to work a lot, but now you can take me every day. Right?"

"We'll see," Marina said with a smile. She toweled him dry and settled him down for a nap, which he insisted he didn't need. He had barely shut his eyes before his deep breathing told her that he was asleep.

With the movement of the sun, the blanket was now in the shade of a large palm tree. She was grateful for that, as her skin continued to feel unnaturally warm, even hot.

The exertions on the reef, coupled with her restless night, had worn her out as well. She curled up at Billy's side, gazing fondly at the little boy lost in sleep. Before very long, she had joined him.

Andrew found them like that. He had left his office after noticing that the house seemed oddly quiet; he was accustomed to hearing Billy's shouts and laughter as he worked, and he missed them. Having found Marina's note, he took the path down to the beach, scanning the water as he went. When there was no sign of them, he began to be worried, but that quickly vanished as he spied them asleep in the shade.

For a moment he stood unmoving, taking in the sight. They looked so right together, even more so than the day before, when he had seen them walking hand in hand. He was surprised by his son's ready acceptance of her, and even a little resentful of it.

Billy had a three-year-old's normal friendliness, but beneath it was a sense of caution that prevented him from easily giving his trust. Though he had never really known his mother, he was aware that she had gone out of his life suddenly and without warning.

Andrew supposed that he thought other adults might do the same. He had taken pains to assure him that wasn't the case, and he thought Billy believed him, at least as far as he himself was concerned. But when it came to others, even Hildy, he held himself apart. Or he had until Marina came.

In his sleep, the little boy had snuggled closer to her. He lay with his head on her breast, one of her slender arms over him; her ebony hair spread out like a blanket over them both.

Andrew came nearer and frowned. Even in the shadow of the palm tree, he could see that her skin was reddened. He reached out, touched a finger lightly to her bare shoulder and saw her wince.

"Billy," he called softly, urging the little boy to wake up. He did so reluctantly, sitting up to rub his eyes. "Go on back to the house. I'll bring Marina."

"Somethin' wrong?" he murmured.

"It will be all right, but I think she's had too much sun."

She woke as he lifted her, and murmured fitfully. "W-what...?"

"You'll feel better soon," he told her, hoping that he was right. Her eyes closed again, and her head fell back against his shoulder. He had no difficulty carrying her, even up the hill path. He was in good shape, and she weighed no more than she should.

She was hardly aware of him removing her bathing suit, not stirring again until he lowered her into a tub of cool water. For a moment her body stiffened against the shock. But she relaxed quickly, and even smiled at him. "I'm sorry you have to take care of me again," she said softly.

"I'm getting used to it," he murmured dryly, vividly aware that he was anything but used to her nudity. She stirred him so powerfully that he had to take several deep breaths before continuing. His big hands moved over her gently, squeezing out spongefuls of the cool water over her breasts and thighs. The contrast between the skin that had been covered and that which had not was becoming steadily more marked. He blamed him-

self for not having warned her to be careful of the sun,
but wondered at the same time why she hadn't known.

"Billy's used to it," he said. "But you'll have to
wear a sun blocker until you become more accustomed."

"I should have thought of that." Though she hardly
could have, since she had no idea what "that" was.

"You haven't been in the sun much, have you?"
The answer was self-evident, but he was glad of anything to keep his mind off the loveliness of the body
he was ministering to.

"Not much," she agreed, her eyes avoiding his.

"That's hard to do, living in the Caribbean."

She shrugged, not knowing what to say. The gesture
brought her breasts into even greater prominence. His
hand brushed inadvertently against the delicate swelling of a nipple. She watched, fascinated, as a dark flush
spread over his lean cheeks.

"You know," he said thickly, "where this is leading."

The joining. It must be the same for his people as it
was for hers, or very much so. Never lightly done,
never undone. The path to the very heart of life itself.
She had been drawn to it in an abstract way, as was
natural, but never had she been tempted to join with a
particular man. Until now.

Her eyes met his, sea green meeting earth brown,
and she nodded.

Chapter 6

The spirit was willing, if a bit apprehensive. The flesh, however, was another matter altogether.

"Sometimes," Andrew said with a wry smile as he helped her from the tub, "I think Mother Nature has a hell of a sense of humor."

She didn't realize exactly what he meant until he very gently wrapped a towel around her and she almost cried out. Without the cooling water, her skin felt as though it was on fire. The slightest touch was intolerable. Tears were close to falling as she contemplated the mess she had made of things.

"I didn't know," she whispered.

He didn't ask how that was possible, but instead soothed her with a murmur and led her back to the bedroom. He took the towel from her, and she lay down on her stomach, wondering how she would ever be able to sleep. Her back had taken the worst of it;

she could almost feel the fingers of fire creeping under her skin.

A cool, soothing lotion touched her. She sighed and dug her toes into the mattress. His hands were large, the palms slightly callused. Their gentleness was a marvel. After a time her skin ceased to burn. The fire had moved within her, close to the center of her womb.

Next morning, when she woke feeling much improved, its heat still lingered.

"What's 'anium?" Billy asked over breakfast. They had been eating in silence, Marina and Andrew trying not to stare at each other. She thought they might as well have saved themselves the effort. They were drawn together as surely as the sun dipped into the ocean. It was as though the joining had already begun.

They became aware of silence, and of Billy watching them. "Xanium's a new element," Andrew said hastily. "That is, it was discovered recently."

"The man on television said it's a piece, but he didn't say a piece of what."

His father looked blank for a moment, then laughed. "For peace, Billy. That's what he must have said. There are some people who think it can be used to build a sort of shield against things like missiles. You remember we've talked about them."

He hadn't wanted to, thinking any child Billy's age was too young to even know about nuclear weapons, much less worry about them. But the world thought differently, or so it seemed. Billy had heard so much about them on television that inevitably he'd asked what they were. Andrew had explained as best he could, hoping not to frighten the boy. He wasn't sure whether he had succeeded or not.

"That's what you're doing," Billy said suddenly. "Isn't it?"

"Doing...?" Andrew repeated before the full implications of the question sank in. He hadn't thought that his son knew anything at all about his work, much less that he realized what it was connected to.

"Building the shield," Billy explained. He looked at Marina proudly. "Daddy does the numbers so the other men know how strong to make the different parts and where to put them in the sky."

Marina had been following the conversation with difficulty, not because she didn't understand it, but because she was afraid that she did. It brought to mind certain rumors she had discounted as too horrible to believe.

It was being said that the people outside were savages without the slightest reverence for life. That they had created weapons of such terror as to be beyond comprehension. That they would inevitably destroy themselves, after which the Inner World would rise again, and its people would emerge to retake the earth.

She had always regarded that as no more than the twisted fantasies of people driven by their own inadequacies to imagine that others were even worse. Now she had to wonder if she had been wrong.

"Your work," she said to Andrew, "sounds very important."

"Billy is exaggerating. I'm strictly on the theoretical end, and I'm only one of several dozen physicists chewing over the same problems."

If he meant to disabuse her of any notion about his own significance, he failed. She knew perfectly well that almost all major breakthroughs occurred when a brilliant mind was left free to roam unhindered.

That he would speak no more about his work just then was clear. The same wall of silence she had sensed before had come down over his thoughts. Not that she would have tried to probe them short of the direst necessity. As she had told him, they were private.

Still, she would have dearly loved to know what course they took. He had withdrawn from her into a place where she could not follow. Yet he was pleasant enough, if only for his son's sake. They finished the meal in apparent harmony. Afterward, they followed the pattern set the day before, though this time she took care to protect herself from the sun.

Would that she could protect herself from the man as easily.

It was nightfall before she saw Andrew again. He had put Billy to bed and come back looking distracted. Before she could say anything, he told her that he was going for a walk along the beach. The way he said it made it clear that he wanted to be alone.

Some time passed after he left before the thought came to her. When it did, she realized that she had been evading it all day. If what she had heard that morning was true and the people of the Outer World really did have weapons of terrible destruction, she owed it to her own people to discover how close a shield from them might be. Without that knowledge, contact between the two races could be dangerous indeed.

There was only one way to gain such knowledge. Though she loathed the idea of subterfuge, she felt she had no choice.

The door to Andrew's office wasn't locked. She slipped inside, but didn't turn on any of the lamps.

There was a moon that night, only a sliver, but enough to see by.

His desk was in the center of the room. She approached it gingerly, stepping around the wires that ran from the wall to a cluster of boxes on the desk top. One of them had a screen like that of the television she was becoming accustomed to. She did not make the mistake of assuming that this was the same thing.

Papers were spread out on the desktop. She bent over them, frowning. They were covered with equations, the meaning of which she could not begin to decipher, though at least some of the symbols were familiar. It seemed she had come across another legacy shared by both Andrew's people and her own.

Frustration banished the pleasure she would otherwise have felt at that. Ruefully she remembered her mathematics teacher exhorting her to apply herself more. She had preferred other subjects and had devoted her energies to them. But she suspected that even if she had done otherwise, she would not be able to understand Andrew's notes. They were far too complex for anyone but a similarly gifted scientist to comprehend.

But understanding wasn't always necessary to remembering. She was, after all, a trained observer whose childhood talent for memory had long since been refined into a reliable tool of her profession. With confidence she opened her mind to what lay before her and let it flow through the cells and synapses that would record it as surely as if she had made an exact copy.

When that was done, she turned to go. It was time to contact her brother again. She would tell him what was happening and show him what she had found. He also had the gift and would be able to remember everything. Moreover, he would be able to seek out the few trusted scientists who might be able to decipher her discovery.

She was worrying over the result of that as she headed for the door, only to stop when she saw the figure standing there.

"Looking for something?" Andrew asked. He stood straight and tall, a darker shape against the darkness of the hallway beyond, his big body effectively blocking the only exit. Not that she was foolish enough to think of fleeing. Some things could not be escaped.

"I thought you had gone for a walk," she said.

He took a step forward, enabling her to see him more clearly. He was scowling, for which she could hardly blame him. "I came back," he told her, rather unnecessarily.

"You didn't mean to stay away very long, did you?"

He shook his head. "I thought you might pull something like this, but I hoped I was wrong. Too bad I wasn't."

"If it makes any difference to you, I don't understand what I saw."

He smiled with such a complete lack of humor that her blood chilled. "You can hardly expect me to believe that." He moved farther into the room and shut the door behind him. His hand reached out to flick a switch. The sudden brightness that followed made her blink. "Besides," he added, "it doesn't matter. What counts is that you went for the bait."

He sat down in the chair behind the desk, put his feet up and regarded her almost casually. "Just out of curiosity, who exactly do you work for?"

"No one."

Andrew shook his head almost indulgently. "Don't bother lying. The truth will come out sooner or later."

"That *is* the truth." At least a part of it. The rest had to remain hidden, no matter what he did.

"You must realize," he said, "that with what's at stake here, the authorities won't be too scrupulous about how they interrogate you."

She swallowed against the sudden constriction of her throat and did her best to look unconcerned. "I have no idea what you're talking about."

"Damn you!" He exploded out of his chair, his long limbs uncoiling with whiplike speed. Before she could draw a breath, he was across the room and had taken hold of her. His hands dug into her arms as he all but lifted her off the ground. "Why do you have to be what you are? A liar, a cheat. Who's paying you? What did they hope to gain?"

"I told you," she gasped, fighting against the waves of fear that threatened to engulf her. "There's no one. I don't know what you're talking about. Let me go!"

When he didn't comply at once, she didn't hesitate. Although violence was anathema to her, she was well prepared to defend herself. The touch she used was light and could do no permanent damage, but it knocked him back against the wall, leaving him as stunned by her unexpected skill as he was by the brief instant of pain she had inflicted.

"What in hell...?" he muttered.

Marina turned to go. There were tears in her eyes that she couldn't bear for him to see. Desperately she forced herself not to think of what might have been as she jerked open the door and started down the hallway, only to be stopped by the sound of sobs coming from Billy's room.

Andrew was right behind her. He heard them, too, and cursed under his breath.

"Bad dream," Billy snuffled when they reached his bed. It hadn't occurred to Marina to leave him to his father. Already, in the short time she had known Billy, she had come to love him. That he felt the same way about her was driven home when, from the sanctuary of Andrew's arms, he gave her a watery smile and reached out a hand. "Thought you went away," he said.

Andrew gave her a startled look. His office was far enough down the hall that, with the door closed, Billy shouldn't have been able to hear them arguing. Marina didn't think that he had. Having touched his mind once, in her desperate cry for help, she knew him to be unusually receptive.

Gently she smoothed his tear-stained cheek, all the while thinking frantically. Common sense decreed that she get away as fast as she possibly could. Everything else in her—instinct, emotion, intuition—told her to stay. Not only for Billy's sake, but for Andrew's and her own.

Over the tousled head of the child, the two adults looked at each other. She required no mind link to know what he was thinking. "We have to talk," he said as he settled Billy back down. The little boy was asleep again within minutes, apparently convinced that they would work everything out between them.

"Under normal circumstances," Andrew said when they had left his room, "I wouldn't hesitate to turn you over to security. This project is far too important for me to allow personal feelings to intrude."

"I'm no threat to it," she said quietly.

He gave her a long, hard look. "I wish I could believe that, but you'll have to admit that there's a lot about you that makes no sense."

She couldn't deny it; from his perspective that was undoubtedly true. "I wish it didn't have to be like that."

"But it does?"

Unhappily, she nodded. "I realize that it's an awful lot to ask, but the fact is, there are things I can't tell you, not because they have anything to do with your project, but simply because other people expect me to be…discreet."

"Who are these other people?"

"If I could tell you that, I could tell you the whole story."

He shook his head slowly. "I don't get it. Usually my instincts are top-notch, and they're telling me you're not the criminal type, but—"

"I'm not," she interrupted. "What I'm involved in breaks none of your laws."

"That's an odd way to put it, as though you come from a different country, with different laws."

She was silent, knowing that she was perilously close to revealing what she must not.

He ran a hand through his thick amber hair. "There has to be a solution to this, one I can live with."

"You could…choose to trust me."

"That's asking a hell of a lot, especially after that little performance in my office." As though he had just remembered that, he demanded, "What was that you did to me, anyway?"

"It's a simple form of self-defense. You'll admit you were handling me rather roughly."

"I'm sorry." The apology was sincere. He had never used his strength against a woman before, and was horrified that he had done so with her. But then, she brought out all sorts of impulses he had never felt before.

"I was going to leave," she said softly. "But Billy…complicates things."

The lines around his mouth deepened. "He's formed a strong attachment to you already."

"You resent that."

"Not exactly, but I don't imagine you plan on hanging around here very long one way or the other. So, inevitably, he's going to be hurt."

She had been thinking about that herself, wondering if it was better for her to go now before the situation had a chance to become even more convoluted than it already was. The trouble was that she didn't believe she could tear herself away. Not all the considerable self-discipline she possessed was equal to that task.

"I'd like to stay awhile," she said quietly. "It wouldn't do Billy any good to simply have me disappear."

"No, I suppose not. But, on the other hand, I can't have you wandering around prying into things."

His bluntness made her flush. Already she regretted the impulse that had taken her into his office. "I assure you," she said, calling on all her dignity, "that you needn't be concerned about that."

"You give a great many assurances," he reminded her, "but no proof that they can be relied on."

"You have my word." At home, that would have been more than enough. In fact, to even suggest otherwise would be grounds for the strongest action. But here, such was apparently not the case.

"I need more than that," Andrew said. "As it happens, I've finished one phase of the project I'm working on, and I can't go on to the next until I receive input from several other people. I've got some time on my hands, and I might as well spend it keeping an eye on you."

She shrugged, hoping to convey the impression that his attention meant very little to her. "As you wish."

Her lack of concern didn't fool him. He grinned almost wolfishly as he took a step toward her. "I think I should warn you that there's nothing I like better than solving puzzles."

"Surely," she murmured, "your work provides you with enough of those."

"I've always thought so. Until now." He was closer still, his breath warm on her cheek, his hands infinitely gentle as they stroked lightly up and down her arms. "I can't decide whether you're deliberately being mysterious, or whether there's something you genuinely feel you have to hide. But, either way, I intend to find out."

With a great deal more confidence than she was feeling, she said, "You can certainly try."

His mouth was very close to hers. She stared, fascinated, as his firm lips parted slightly to reveal strong white teeth. "Oh, I will, Marina," he murmured. "You can count on that."

For so large and strong a man, he could be remarkably tender. There was nothing at all rough or intrusive about the touch of his mouth on hers. His lips moved lightly, persuasively, until, with a soft groan, she relaxed and yielded to his embrace.

Slowly he deepened the kiss, his tongue stroking the soft underside of her lower lip, tracing the ridge of her teeth, before engaging hers in play. She discovered quickly that she loved the taste of him, a combination of mint and the tart red wine they had shared at dinner. A soft moan escaped her as she ran her hands over the broad expanse of his back, feeling through the cotton shirt the reflexive bunching of his muscles.

He broke off the kiss to gaze down at her for a moment. His eyes were hooded, their expression unreadable, but she looked back at him without fear. Against her lower body, she could feel his arousal. Without thought, her hips moved, wringing a groan from him.

"Don't do that," he muttered in the instant before his mouth closed over hers again. This time he was less gentle, with an undercurrent of hunger that excited her deeply. She met him touch for touch, with a skill that should have surprised her but didn't. With Andrew, all things felt right.

At last, when the fire leaping between them threatened to burn out of control, Andrew lifted his head and glared down at her. She had to stifle a laugh at his male anger and bewilderment. "I must be out of my mind," he muttered. "For all I know, you're a spy."

"Don't start that again," she whispered, pulling his head back down to her. The kiss she initiated literally took his breath away. He felt as though his very soul was being drawn out of his body.

She was light and heat in his arms, strength to match his own, and beauty beyond any he had ever dreamed of possessing. In a world that was too often full of disappointments, hers was a promise of ecstasy he could not resist. Whatever the mystery about her, he would worry about it later.

Chapter 7

Marina didn't remember Andrew carrying her down the hallway to his room. She barely noticed when he lowered her onto the bed and followed her down, covering her body swiftly with his own. All that mattered was that he stay close to her, as close as he could possibly get.

"Again," she murmured when his mouth brushed over her taut breast. "Please...."

He was delighted to comply, even though it was sweet torture to touch her like that with the barrier of their clothes still in place. Her frankness about her needs led him to imagine that she was very experienced, and he didn't hesitate to give vent to his desires. Her soft, slender body beneath his was a provocation he could not withstand. First slowly, then with greater and greater urgency, he kissed and caressed every part of her that he could reach.

Her long, slim throat knew the touch of his mouth,

as did the sweet hollow between her collarbones and the shadowed cleft that separated her breasts. His hands cupped her lightly, the thumbs rubbing slowly over her rigid nipples, before passing on to gently take the measure of her narrow waist. Her flat belly drew in sharply as his long, blunt-tipped fingers brushed over it. He held her hips lightly, rubbing his palms against them for several moments before reaching round to grasp her buttocks and lift her more firmly against him.

His head was buried against her breasts, his powerful thighs thrust between her slim legs, every inch of his body vividly imprinting itself on hers. She cried out softly, all but mindless with need. It was too much; she couldn't possibly endure this and survive.

"No more," she gasped as he raised his head and she saw the smoky light burning in his eyes.

"A moment ago," he reminded her tautly, his own breath coming in labored gasps, "you wanted more."

"I can't stand this."

"Neither can I," he admitted, abruptly pulling her up so that she was sitting on the bed, facing him. His touch was gentle again, if a bit clumsy, as he rapidly undid the buttons of her blouse. Her breasts swelled over the cups of her bra, her hardened nipples clearly visible through the thin lace.

The bra had a front closing. His hands trembled as he undid it and pushed it aside to reveal her completely. "You're lovely!" he murmured before leaning forward to let his mouth take possession of the treasure he had found.

Marina thought she would go mad from the sensations he evoked. She was lost in a whirlpool of throbbing need. Her body was on fire for him. Never in her life had she imagined that she could yearn so intensely for something that she would feel pain at its absence. All thought of the problems they faced was blanked out as she reached for him.

With fumbling urgency and shared laughter, their clothes were at last removed. Raised as she had been in a society that venerated the human body as the highest expression of beauty, Marina had no self-consciousness about her nudity. But the heat in Andrew's gaze made her flush, not with shyness, but with excitement so intense that she could hardly bear it.

Her eyes ran over him hungrily, taking in the broad expanse of his shoulders and chest, the curls of dark hair that spread out between his flat nipples, narrowing into a thin line between his rib cage and across his muscled abdomen, flowering again at his groin, where his manhood nestled. The point of her tongue slipped between her teeth as she studied him. He was magnificently male in his nakedness. Tall and clean of limb, a statue brought to vivid, thrilling life.

Her mouth curved in a smile of eternal femininity as she lifted her arms and held them out to him.

He needed no further invitation. Her name was a prayer on his lips as he bore her back down onto the bed. Their limbs entwined, their mouths stroking, tongues licking, they drove each other higher and higher.

Marina writhed helplessly beneath him. The rough silk of his skin rubbing against her soft smoothness stunned her. She had had no idea that her body could feel so much, more than it seemed possible to survive. There had to be an end, and soon. No wonder, she thought dazedly, that people spoke so reverently of the joining. It was a force as primeval as that which had created life itself, and to take it lightly would be the height of foolishness.

She did not, nor, she sensed, did Andrew. His labored breathing matched her own. In the dim light she could see that his taut features were honed by passion. He moved, and she gasped as his manhood probed between her thighs.

Then she was opening to him, both body and mind. Liquid heat spiraled through her. The tears she had fought so hard to deny earlier that evening could no longer be restrained. They spilled from her sea-green eyes, down her pale cheeks, to be caught on the tip of his tongue.

At the hot, salty taste of her, his last hold on self-control broke. With a low, inarticulate cry, he thrust into her, feeling the sweet, welcoming tightness engulf him completely. Only then, when he was fully within her, did a flicker of remembered sensation make him start.

"Marina," he murmured, gazing down at her, "why didn't you tell me?"

The smile she gave him captured the essence of femininity in a single, enthralling instant. "I was afraid you would hold back."

"I would have. I don't want to hurt you."

"You didn't," she assured him, at the same time raising her hips slightly.

His reaction was eminently satisfactory. He gasped, and his eyes closed for a moment, only to glitter with the hard brightness of steel when he looked at her again. "For heaven's sake, don't."

"I must." There was no other way she could explain it to him, or even to herself. All she knew was that she had to have him completely, or the hunger he had awakened would destroy her.

Her hips rose again, her body tightening around him, and this time he made no attempt to resist. He was beyond rational thought, engulfed in sensation, yet still able to think of her well-being before his own. Slowly, then with increasing strength, he thrust into her again and again. She met him fully, matching his rhythm until their bodies moved as one.

Higher and higher they climbed toward a shattering peak of fulfillment. At the last instant, as they tumbled over it and fell into a haven of radiant light, Marina's mind reached out to his. She could no more stop herself from doing so than she could cease to breathe. For her it was as integral a part of the joining as the union of their bodies.

In an instant when time itself seemed to splinter, their spirits merged and for an infinity were truly one.

Andrew woke several hours later. It was dark in the room, and he felt strangely confused, as though uncertain not only of where but of *who* he was. It took several moments for him to regain his equilibrium. When he did, he sat up slowly and looked at the woman asleep beside him.

It appeared that no dreams disturbed her rest. She slept soundly, her lips slightly parted and her breasts, covered by the sheet, rising and falling slowly. Dark lashes lay against cheeks that were still slightly flushed. He stared at her and remembered.

What had happened to him? He knew their lovemaking had been magnificent, despite his shock at finding her a virgin. He had never experienced such incredible pleasure with any woman, hadn't even

suspected that it existed. But that aside, there had been
something else, at the end, that he thought he must
surely have imagined.

Lacking words to describe it even to himself, he
shook his head in confusion. It was as though he felt
the faint echoes of Marina's presence within his mind,
as he felt his within hers. But that didn't really begin
to describe it. Rather than grasp the feelng itself, he
could only recognize its effects. He felt as though he
was no longer alone.

Why that should be so he could not imagine. He had
never felt particularly lonely. Solitude had never troubled him; he had always been content with his own
company. Yet there had been times when, in some
careless moment of speculation, he had caught a
glimpse of a vastness so immense as to be terrifying.
Then he had known, though he swiftly shied away from
it, how small and vulnerable a man was, and how desperate the need for shelter against the cold emptiness.

There were those who believed that hell was a place
of writhing flames; Andrew thought otherwise. He was
more inclined to agree with the ancient Norsemen, who
had imagined perdition to be a place of endless ice and
frost. Man was born of the fire that lurked at the heart
of the stars themselves; it was the absence of it that
destroyed him.

For a moment longer he thought back over what had
happened between himself and Marina, trying to understand it. The harder he attempted to grasp the memory, the more it slipped away from him. Fearing that
he might lose it altogether, he gave up the attempt and
lay back down beside her. She murmured in her sleep
and turned toward him. After the barest hesitation, he
gathered her into his arms.

* * *

As though Billy sensed the change in Marina and his father's relationship, he was quiet and watchful that morning. As she prepared breakfast, Marina tried to coax a smile from him, but he would have none of it. His large brown eyes, so like his father's, followed her around the kitchen. Seated at the table, he banged his feet back and forth against the chair railing and kept a firm hold on his blanket. When she set a cup of juice and a slice of melon in front of him, he ignored them.

"Billy," she asked gently, "is something wrong?"

His lower lip trembled. Glumly, he shook his head.

"Please tell me," she said, bending down beside him. Softly, she reached out a hand and stroked his hair. He jerked away from her and, as he did so, tears spilled from his eyes.

Instantly she had her arms around him and was holding him close. His sturdy little body was stiff with resistance for a moment, but he relaxed quickly and snuggled his head into her shoulder.

"You aren't still upset about the dream you had last night, are you?" she asked.

When he didn't answer, she tilted his head back and looked at him closely. "Tell me the truth now, Billy. Is it the dream that's bothering you, or something else?"

So softly that she could barely hear him, he murmured, "Daddy."

His father? For a moment Marina wondered if he could somehow be aware of what had passed between her and Andrew, and be disturbed by it. But aside from the fact that he had been deeply asleep at the time, she doubted he was old enough to be concerned by such things. Still, there was no getting around the fact that something had him tied up in knots.

"Tell me," she urged gently. "I'll do whatever I can to help."

The look he gave her, hopefulness undercut by doubt, wrung her heart. Slowly, he said, "I know a secret."

"You do? Well...do you want to tell me what it is?"

"You know, too. Only Daddy doesn't."

"You and I know something your father doesn't? That's what has you worried?"

Silently, he nodded. She cast her mind back over the days they had spent together, trying to imagine what it was that Billy imagined he knew. She could think of several things, but none of them could legitimately be called a secret.

A possibility rippled at the back of her mind. She tensed, but forced herself to speak gently. "Billy, how long have you known this secret?"

"Since the storm. I heard you."

She had taken such care to touch his mind as lightly as she possibly could that she hadn't thought he remembered the encounter. It appeared she had been mistaken.

"I told Daddy it was Momma," he explained. "Then I said it was you. He didn't un'erstand. Me neither, but now I figured it out." He looked rather proud of himself as he added, "You made my lamb smile, so's I wouldn't be afraid."

She had done that, finding in his mind an object that gave him comfort and turning it to her own uses. At the time it had seemed the right thing to do. She had been, after all, in danger of losing her life. But now, seeing the turmoil she had caused, she wished she had found another way.

"It's a secret, isn't it?" he asked.

What could she say to him? If she asked him not to tell his father, she would be placing an unfair burden on him. And if he did tell Andrew about the lamb, there was a chance his father would write it off as imagination and forget about it.

But there was also a possibility that he would stick it away in the back of his mind, mull it over and eventually realize that there might be some connection between what his son said and his own experience of the night before. If he did, he would be that much closer to discovering her true identity.

"Billy," she said slowly, "I appreciate that you don't want to do anything that would hurt me, even by accident."

He looked relieved that she understood his problem, but still uncertain as to what she wanted him to do. She dropped a light kiss on his forehead and stood up, saying as she did so, "Secrets are fine, but you shouldn't feel that you have to keep anything from your father. He loves you, and there's nothing you could tell him that he wouldn't understand."

"But it's your secret, too."

"Yes," she agreed, unable to lie to him. "But I still don't want you to feel you can't tell your father something because of me."

"You could tell him," he pointed out, not unreasonably. "Then it would be his secret, too."

"I'm afraid it's...a little complicated."

"You said he'd understand."

Despite herself, she smiled. Billy might only be three, but he had all his father's intelligence, and there was nothing wrong with how he put it to use. "The problem," she said as simply as she could, "is that the secret you and I know, about how I made the lamb smile and called to you, involves a bigger secret that belongs to a whole lot of other people. If I tell it, I'll be breaking a promise to them."

"And you'll get in trouble?"

"Well...I don't imagine they'd be too happy with me."

"Daddy can keep secrets, too."

"But he might not want to keep this one. You feel you need to tell him about the lamb, and he might feel the same way about the bigger secret. There might be someone he thought he had to tell."

He thought that over, then nodded slowly. "Soon it wouldn't be a secret at all."

"That's the problem exactly."

Having said all she could, she went back to fixing breakfast. When she looked at Billy again he had dug into his melon and was eating it with relish. But his eyes were still thoughtful.

Andrew joined them a few minutes later. He hadn't seen Marina since rising that morning and discovering that she had left the bed before him. On his way to the kitchen he had been detoured by a phone call from David Longfellow, which he'd only just concluded. The memory of it still rankled, and he was frowning as he came through the door.

The frown faded as he saw her standing by the counter, a look of uncertainty in her eyes and a slight flush staining her cheeks. The memory of how it had been between them darted through him. To his amusement, but hardly his surprise, he felt his body tighten in response. Quickly he turned to Billy, gave him a smile and said, "How would you both like to go fishing today?"

"Oh, boy!" Billy exclaimed. "Fishing!"

"Marina?" Andrew asked.

"That would be fine. I'll pack a lunch."

Her self-consciousness had faded by the time they left the house for the drive to the harbor. Instead she felt only a warm glow of happiness that increased each time her eyes met Andrew's.

Billy skipped ahead of them along the pier. Marina was checking automatically to be sure he didn't go too far when something about him struck her notice.

"Do you see?" she asked Andrew. "He hasn't got his blanket."

"I know. He left it at home."

"You didn't say anything?"

He shook his head. "I didn't want to make a big thing about it. It's never really bothered me that he needed it to feel secure; lots of kids go through that. But it won't hurt him to outgrow it, which he seems to be doing."

He didn't add, though he could have, that the coincidence of Billy forgetting his blanket almost immediately after Marina's arrival hadn't surprised him. As the boy's father, he would have liked to believe that he provided all the security Billy needed. But he was honest enough to admit that wasn't necessarily the case. Billy responded to Marina in a different way, perhaps simply because she was a very warm and loving woman—as Andrew himself had good reason to know.

At the end of the pier a gleaming white trimaran rode at anchor, its triple hull swaying on the outgoing tide. Marina stopped to admire it. Her experience with such vessels was limited to photographs, drawings and a few precious sightings. On their first trip to the harbor she had longed to take a closer look, but had been afraid such behavior might seem odd. Surely anyone who said she had grown up in the islands would take boats for granted.

But now, confronted with the exquisitely graceful craft, she could not resist. "It's lovely," she said. "An ingenious design, light but strong."

"You're familiar with trimarans?" Andrew asked.

"Not...exactly. I've never been on one before."

"That's easily remedied." Before she could protest, he stepped lightly from the dock onto the boat and held out a hand for her to follow. As he did so, he called to Billy, who was busy peering over the side of the dock into the blue-green water, where a school of minnows was darting about. The little boy jumped onto the boat, apparently without a second thought.

"This is yours?" Marina asked, impressed despite herself.

Andrew nodded. "I picked her up a couple of years ago. She was in for an engine repair when we were here before, but that's all taken care of, so I thought we'd let her get the kinks out."

The way he spoke of the boat, as though it was a woman, startled Marina, but she accepted it as a sign of his great affection for his vessel. She could hardly blame him. At first glance the *Sea Witch* was magnificent, and greater familiarity only served to increase that impression.

Once they were away from the small harbor Andrew gave her a quick rundown on the rudiments of sailing. He had realized that she knew nothing about it, but didn't find that odd. There were a great many people in the islands who never even set foot on a boat, much less knew how to operate one. Marina was fascinated by the way the wind could be harnessed to provide power. She quickly grasped the basics of tacking and even took a turn at the wheel, though she was clearly glad to relinquish it before very long.

While he took a southwesterly course away from Angle Key, Billy showed her around below. The little boy was an intrepid sailor and told his father in her presence that he would prefer to live at sea rather than on land.

"Don't you think that would be neat, Marina? You could go swimming whenever you wanted and make friends with all the fish."

"That sounds great," she allowed with a smile as she put away the food she had packed. The galley held a small refrigerator, a microwave oven and cabinets well filled with staples. She realized with some surprise that it would be possible to stay afloat on such a vessel for quite a long time, and wondered if anyone in the Outer World did so.

"But if you did live at sea, Billy, wouldn't you miss the land?"

He thought about that for a moment, then shrugged. "I guess. It's nice, too. Having both is best."

She was beginning to think so, too, which could only lead her to even more dangerous thoughts. Closing the refrigerator door, she said, "Let's go back upstairs and see if your dad would like a drink."

He giggled and looked at her from between his fingers. "You mean topside. Upstairs's landlubber talk."

"Pardon me," she said with mock solemnity. "Topside it is."

Billy scrambled on ahead of her; she followed more slowly, wanting to take in all the details that she possibly could. Theseus would be fascinated by this vessel. That reminded her that she had to get back in touch with him and find out what was going on with the council. Despite the warmth of the sun that greeted her when she stepped out on deck, she shivered. It was foolhardy to try to pretend that the situation was any better than it was, yet the temptation to do so was all but irresistible.

She looked at Andrew, seated behind the wheel. He had taken his shirt off, and she found herself unable to keep from staring at his broad shoulders and chest. His skin was tanned to a shade similar to that of the chased bronze cups that sat on her mother's table. Yet unlike the bronze, it was enticingly warm to the touch. She remembered that even as now-familiar heat darted through her body.

Beside Andrew, Billy's skin was far softer and lighter. The little boy leaned against his father, who had an arm around his shoulders. Unaware as yet of her presence, they were deep in talk about the intricacies of the compass that Andrew was showing to his son.

Marina's throat tightened as a sweet but painful yearning filled her. She longed to be able to go to Andrew without hesitation or reserve, to share with him the pleasure and the responsibility of teaching Billy, and to know that the close of day would find them together. But that was not the case, and as she listened to the waves lapping against the *Sea Witch*'s triple hull, she couldn't help but think of what lay beneath them.

Chapter 8

"It's simple," Andrew said. "You bait the hook, then release the reel, keeping your finger there to hold the line. Cast it out...that's right, good. Now, just wait until you feel a tugging, give it a good jerk and reel it in."

Marina nodded without daring to take her eyes off the fishing rod. When Andrew had mentioned going fishing, she had thought of the huge nets she had occasionally seen in the higher reaches of the sea above the Inner World. Theseus had explained their use to her, not sparing his contempt.

The nets were indiscriminate; they trapped not only food fish but also other forms of sea life, which were then callously killed and tossed back into the water. More than once Theseus had led raids to cut the nets. Even those on the council, including Uncle Orestes, who disapproved of any contact with the Outer World tolerated such actions because they helped to maintain good relations with the dolphins and porpoises who were most often the nets' inadvertent victims.

She had wondered if that was what Andrew intended to do and, if he did, how she could stand by and watch. It was with great relief that she realized the rod and reel could catch far fewer fish and then only those that chose to take the bait. And, it seemed, even some of those could escape.

"I've got something," she cried, excited despite herself. Quickly she gave the rod a sharp tug, as he had shown her, then reeled in the line, only to discover as the hook came clear of the water that it was empty. Not only was there no fish, but the bait had disappeared.

"Don't feel bad," Andrew said when he saw her disappointment. "It happens all the time. Try to be faster when you think you've got a bite."

The next time she did and succeeded in landing a small—admittedly very small—bass. "Sorry," Andrew said, deftly removing the hook from its mouth. "This isn't a keeper. Better to throw it back and let it grow up." He suited his action to his words, explaining, "That's what helps to maintain the fish population."

She nodded, in full agreement with him. "That one won't even lay eggs for several months yet. It would have been a shame to take her."

He straightened up and gave her a puzzled look, one that didn't completely conceal his enjoyment at her appearance. At his insistence, over her bathing suit she was wearing an old white shirt that had belonged to him. It came halfway down her thighs and inevitably drew his eyes to the expanse of silken flesh left exposed beneath the hem. Flesh he had personally made sure was covered with a sun blocker. Her comfort aside, there was no way he was going to let her get burned again, leaving him to expire from frustration.

"What makes you think it was a female?" he asked absently, far more interested in her than he was in the fish. Rather ruefully, he suspected that it would have taken nothing less than Moby Dick himself to distract him.

Marina was about to say that anyone could plainly see the bass's gender when she realized that he couldn't. He knew how to fish, and even felt the need to respect what he caught, but he didn't have the awareness of the various species that she had possessed since childhood.

Quickly she said, "There's a fifty-fifty chance, isn't there?"

"Oh, I don't know," he said with a grin. "Maybe better than that. She had a certain look about her." He glanced over to where Billy had fallen asleep on an inflatable mattress. The little boy looked as though nothing short of a circus band marching through would rouse him. Satisfied that they were unobserved, Andrew took a step toward Marina.

She caught the gleam in his eyes and laughed, playfully brandishing the rod. "Oh, no, none of that. We're here to fish, remember?"

His smile deepened as he kept on advancing. "I'm a steak and potatoes man myself."

"If you're hungry, I packed a big lunch."

"It can wait. Come here."

She laughed, enjoying the game. It was the first time she had played it, and it pleased her to think that something as awe inspiring as the joining could be accompanied by such lighthearted humor. "What if I don't?" she asked provocatively.

"I guess I'll have to come after you." He did, until she was gently but inextricably backed into the bulkhead. He took the rod from her, propped it up on the deck and leaned his hands on either side of her. "Now, what was that you said about being hungry?"

She opened her mouth to answer, only to have whatever she might have said go clean out of her head. All she could think of was his nearness, the hard lines of his body and the heat of his burnished skin. "I forget," she murmured, unconsciously touching the tip of her tongue to her parted lips.

Andrew groaned deep in his throat. A breeze blew up, fluttering the ebony strands that hung to her waist. She had tied her hair back with a bit of yarn she had found in the kitchen. In a previous incarnation it had been used to decorate a birthday present for Billy. His father thought it was doing rather better for itself now.

Without taking his eyes from her, he twined her hair around his hand, drawing her ever closer to him. It felt like warm silk against his fingers. He remembered the touch of her the night before and was not ashamed of the tremor that raced through him. "This morning I wanted to tell you how beautiful you are. I was disappointed to find you gone, but I don't think I would have been able to find the words anyway."

She swallowed and, drawing on her courage, said, "I think you're beautiful, too."

The corners of his mouth rose. "I've been called a lot of things, but never that."

She sensed that he was slightly embarrassed by it, but nonetheless pleased. Feeling rather daring, she touched him lightly, tracing the contours of his perfectly defined shoulders with something akin to wonder.

"Don't do that," he muttered, grasping hold of her hand. "There are a lot of hours yet until night."

"It's hard for me as well," she admitted.

That was more than he needed to hear. At the realization that she desired him as much as he did her, his already taut body grew even more so. A muscle leaped in his jaw as he bent his head and lightly raked his mouth over hers. "So much innocence," he murmured thickly, "and so much wisdom. How do you combine the two?"

Her eyes, green as the sea at dawn, widened. She had thought that last night she had felt everything there was to feel, but now she suspected that was not the case. Her body tingled with a new awareness. Like him, she glanced at the sky and grudged the sun the remaining hours of its passage.

The blameless cause of their frustration awoke a short time later. Billy sat up, rubbed his eyes and declared that he was starving. Glad to have something to do, Marina prepared lunch, then took another try at fishing. Expecting a gentle tug on the line, she was unprepared for the wrench that strained her arms.

"Good lord!" she exclaimed. "What's that?"

"Dinner," Andrew said succinctly. "Easy now, give him some line; let him wear himself out."

"I'm not sure I can—"

"You can do it, Marina," Billy said. "I know you can. C'mon!"

Thus encouraged, she strained on the rod, slowly feeding line out and reeling it in as Andrew guided her. A fine sheen of sweat broke out all over her, and her breath came in labored gasps, as much from excitement as from the exertion. But at last, just when she thought she couldn't possibly hold out any longer, a dark shape broke the surface of the water.

"That's it," Andrew said. "Steady now." He leaned far over the side of the boat and deftly maneuvered a net at the end of a long pole. After snagging the fish in it, he presented it to her proudly. "That's the granddaddy of groupers. We could feed an army on him."

The fish, now safely expired, had the thick, rough hide typical of its kind, but Marina knew its flesh would be sweet. She couldn't help being pleased with herself. "I actually did it!"

"Of course you did," Andrew said as he removed the fish from her line and tossed it into a large pail of water. "Didn't you think you could?"

"Well…I have to admit, I had my doubts."

"That was easy compared to the next step."

"What's that?" she asked cautiously.

"Cleaning it," Billy chimed in, making a face that made clear what he thought of that.

"Oh, that's nothing," Marina said. "Give it here; I'll do it now."

Andrew looked at her skeptically. "It's okay, I was just kidding. I'll clean it for you."

"You really don't have to," she insisted. "I know how to do it, and I don't mind." In fact, she was willing to bet she was more adept at the task than he was. Which, now that she thought about it, might not be a good thing to reveal. "Of course, if you'd prefer to do it yourself…"

Andrew assured her that he did, and the matter was dropped. They had raised anchor and were heading back to Angle Key an hour or so later when Billy suddenly pointed toward the horizon.

"What's that?" he asked.

His father looked in the same direction and shook his head. "I don't know. I've never seen a boat equipped like that."

"Can I see through the binoculars?"

"I guess so. Here." He handed them to Billy, who looked through them for a moment before giving them back. "Funny boat. You look."

Andrew did, and Marina saw his puzzlement deepen. "It says *Questor* on the prow, out of New York."

"Atlantis," Marina murmured before she could stop herself.

"What's that?" Andrew asked.

"It was in the paper…about the scientists who are searching for Atlantis. The name of their vessel is *Questor*."

"Well I'll be." Andrew chuckled. "Don't tell me they think it's around here?"

"Can we look for it, too?" Billy urged.

"I don't think so." His father inclined his head toward the pail where the grouper lay. "We've got a better chance of getting that fish to talk than of finding Atlantis."

Andrew was still chuckling as he guided the *Sea Witch* back to the dock. Marina, on the other hand, found nothing whatsoever to be amused about.

That night, while Andrew put Billy to bed, she stepped out onto the patio. The sky was clouding over, but the air was very calm; there was no sign of another storm approaching. The stars were hidden from her, and the moon was no more than a mist-wreathed hint of itself. Tree frogs filled the darkness with their steady, high-pitched calls. She inhaled the lingering fragrances of bougainvillea and jacaranda, and sought vainly for some semblance of peace within herself.

Theseus would be sure to sense the lack of it. He would worry and, inevitably, ask questions she could not answer. Yet she couldn't delay contacting him any longer. Besides needing the information he could provide, she loved him far too much to leave him in suspense about her fate.

Slowly, with more effort than she had ever had to exert before, she gathered herself inward, formed a single thought until it was a clear, sharp ray and sent it beaming into the darkness. She knew the path well, since it was with Theseus that she had first perfected her skill at such communication. As children, they had practiced on each other and ultimately had become equally adept.

It was a talent shared by all the people of the Inner World, who were nonetheless aware that it had not been theirs originally. They theorized that nature had provided it as a response to the extreme danger they faced. Whether or not that was correct, the fact was that the mind blend was the simplest and surest form of communication they possessed. Unless it was blocked.

At first she didn't understand what had gone wrong. It was as though her mind had run up against a stone wall. The experience was shocking and even somewhat painful. Instinctively she drew back and tried to discover what had happened. On the chance that she had done something wrong—as unlikely as that was—she tried again, only to encounter the same problem. Only then did she suspect the cause.

A cold chill ran through her as her stomach muscles clenched. There was only one way she knew of to prevent such communication, and it was used only in the most extreme cases. In a remote part of the Inner

World, a place where very few ever ventured willingly, there was a place called the Citadel. In it were confined the small number of people given to committing crimes. To prevent them from using the mind link to create further mischief, they were kept in rooms carved out of rock crystal, the only substance known to be impenetrable to thoughts.

It was against such a place that her mind had to stop. No wonder she felt bruised and dazed. Far more than that, though, she was desperately worried about Theseus. She could only imagine what had led to his arrest and incarceration, and how he must be faring in such a terrible place. That she was the cause of his suffering was a torment she almost could not bear. A soft moan broke from her as she wrapped her arms around herself and doubled over, driven by her pain.

"Marina!" Andrew's voice penetrated her dazed state. She looked up to find him staring at her with deep concern. "What's wrong? Are you hurt?"

She shook her head quickly, forcing herself to drop her arms to her sides. "No, I'm all right. I was just... thinking."

"What about?" he asked more softly as he came to her. Moonlight bathed the chiseled planes and angles of his face; the effect should have been harsh, but instead she was aware only of the gentleness in him.

"About home," she murmured. It was true enough. Theseus was a vital part of home to her. She could not imagine it without him.

"You miss it."

She nodded. "I suppose that's natural."

He touched her cheek lightly with the back of his hand. "I can't lie to you, Marina. Whatever is keeping you here, I'm glad of it."

"So am I," she said, struck even as she did so by how true that was. The thought of leaving him was equally as painful as her longing for home, and the fact that she had known him only a few days didn't matter. They were joined, and in some way he would remain with her forever. But that was not enough. She wanted not only the memory of him, but the strong, solid reality.

A dozen questions clamored in Andrew's mind. He still longed to solve the mystery of her. That she could withhold something so elemental as the truth about who she was bothered him deeply. After what they had shared, it seemed to him that there should be only trust and openness between them. But he sensed that to try to probe beyond the boundaries she had established would achieve nothing, except to make her sadder and more tense than she already was. That was something he could not bring himself to do.

Instead, he wanted to banish the shadows from her eyes and replace them with joy.

His hands touched her back lightly, stroking between her shoulder blades and up to the nape of her neck, where he could feel the tightness in her muscles. "You're very tense. Come inside and I'll give you a back rub."

"You want to do more than that," she said quite distinctly. There was a desperation in her—born of her fear for Theseus and her pain at being torn between her home and this man. It provoked her not so much to hurt him in turn as to make clear to him that she knew where they stood. Sentimentality, romanticism, illusion, all these things were not for them.

He winced, and she regretted the words, though she still would not have withdrawn them. "It's true," he said. "I want to make love with you. Is there something wrong with that?"

She lowered her head, unable to meet his eyes any longer. "No…nothing wrong. I want it, too."

"But the thought of it still makes you unhappy?"

"Not really." She leaned toward him, resting her head on his chest, and listened to the steady beat of his heart. "I would be far more unhappy if we couldn't be together again. It's only that…"

"That you know you'll be leaving, if not tomorrow, then the next day, or the next?"

"Yes…that's it."

His arms came around her, cradling her close. She felt his head resting on hers, the tenderness of his mouth brushing her hair. "You don't have to leave, you know. You could simply choose to stay."

"There would be nothing simple about such a choice." In fact, though she could not say so to him, the implications of any such decision were all but inconceivable. It was bad enough that she had violated the laws of her world to enter his. For her to even contemplate staying defied all reason. If nothing else, it would defeat her purpose: to return with information that would convince her people that such contact was desirable. For that she had risked her own life and placed her brother in terrible jeopardy.

"I can't imagine," Andrew said, "having you walk away without my knowing why you thought it necessary."

Unconsciously, she rubbed her cheek against his shirt, feeling the cool roughness of the cotton stretched tautly over the velvet hardness beneath. Everything in her cried out to tell him the truth. But she feared what she would face if she did. Beyond the betrayal of her

own honor that telling him would entail, she dreaded
the thought that he wouldn't believe her and that, by
the time she finally convinced him, he would see her
as some sort of freak with whom the mere thought of
intimacy was distasteful, let alone the reality.

Part of her mind refused to think him capable of such
a judgment, but doubt lingered. It was bad enough that
she had to lose him eventually; to lose his esteem first
would be unbearable.

"Forget what's to come," she whispered against his
heated skin. Her hands reached up, her fingers fumbling slightly, to undo the buttons of his shirt, and slide
between them. Lightly she stroked the silken whorls of
hair beneath which hard muscle leaped and rippled.
"We have this moment. It can be...golden." As
golden as the light exploding behind her eyes, drawing
her down into wild, sweet languor. Her blood ran like
warm honey through her veins. She lifted her head and
stared at him with eyes heavy-lidded and slumberous
with passion.

He made a low, hard sound, part curse, part prayer,
and lifted her into his arms. The distance from the patio
to the house was short. Inside, he carried her swiftly
down the hallway as he had the night before, but this
time he didn't lay her down on the bed. Instead, he
placed her gently on her feet and stepped back to look
at her.

"Undress for me, Marina."

The taut command in his voice made her breathless.
For a moment she could not obey. Then, slowly, she
undid the first button of her shirt...the second...the
third...and so on until the last fell open. Holding his
eyes, she slipped the shirt from her shoulders and let
it drop to the floor.

When they had come home from fishing, she had removed her bathing suit and afterward had not bothered with a bra. Above the white cotton slacks she wore, she was naked. Her breasts were full and high, the nipples erect. By comparison, her waist was startlingly small. Andrew thought about running his mouth over her, and his nostrils flared.

"The rest," he said thickly.

The slacks had a tie belt, which she undid with maddening concentration. She was discovering, to her own surprise, that she liked putting on this little show for him. It made her feel deliciously bold and seductive, but more than that, it gave her a sense of control, which, just then, she sorely needed. In the back of her mind she wondered if he might not be one step ahead of her and have already thought of that. She wouldn't put it past him, but then, from the look in his eyes, she had to conclude that absolutely anything was possible.

"You have magnificent legs," he murmured when she had slipped the slacks off and stood before him in nothing but a lacy scrap of panties. "Beautifully shaped and with just the right amount of muscle. What accounts for such perfection, do you think?"

"I...uh...swim a lot," she said, watching the muscle leap in his clenched jaw. It was a very odd sensation to stand almost nude before a more or less fully clothed man. She felt almost unbearably vulnerable, yet, paradoxically, not at all afraid.

"Wonderful exercise, swimming," he said as he placed both his strong hands on her hips and drew her to him. "Great for the heart."

"Hmm." Not very articulate, but it was all she was capable of at the moment.

His fingers had slipped beneath the elastic edges of

her panties. Gently, he eased them down, over the legs he had praised. As he did so, he knelt, clasping her around the buttocks with one hand as, with the other, he removed her last garment. When it was gone, he did not stand up immediately, but instead pressed his face to her silken belly and slowly rubbed his mouth back and forth.

Marina's head fell back. She moaned helplessly and tried to clutch at him. He stymied her by grasping both her wrists with his hand. His arm tightened around her as he continued his exquisite ministrations. "I want you on fire for me," he rasped. "Whatever happens in the future, you'll remember this night forever."

Dazedly, she thought that he already had his wish. If they were somehow to be parted right then, the memory of what they had already shared would be burned into her forever. But there was more—much more—to come. He rose with fluid grace, but did not release her hands.

She continued a willing prisoner, as he lightly touched each of her breasts in turn, lingering on the upthrust nipples. "Lovely," he murmured as he bent his head and slowly suckled her. Heat coiled in her womb, a living thing demanding release. She sobbed and tried to reach for him again.

He let go of her wrists, allowing her to tangle her hands in his thick hair, but not even her most urgent tugging would compel him to lift his head. Instead he continued to lave her nipples with his tongue and draw them into the moist heat of his mouth until, after long, sweet moments, her knees gave way.

She would have fallen if he hadn't moved with light-ning speed to catch her. Supported by his strength, she slipped off his shirt and ran her hands down his chest until they encountered the snap of his jeans. The merest flicker of shyness made her hesitate, only to vanish when he pressed against her palm and she felt the urgency of his desire.

Tenderly, with exquisite care, she revealed him to her touch. His masculinity fascinated her; it was the perfect complement to her femininity. For long, delightful moments she stroked and caressed him until at last he could bear no more.

"You'll unman me," he said with a tender smile as he lifted her onto the bed.

She laughed a bit shakily, on fire with need for him. "I don't think that's possible."

Gently he parted her thighs and teased their inner flesh. She bit her lip to hold back her cries and stared down at his hand, so dark against her opalescence. "Andrew...please..."

"Tell me what you want, sweet Marina."

"You...now. Don't make me wait any longer."

"I don't think I could," he murmured as he spread her legs wider and moved between them. "Even if I wanted to."

On the last syllable, he entered her. His thrust was hard and deep, taking her completely even as he gave himself without reserve. Her hips arched, and her nails dug into his back. They moved as one, perfectly matched in rhythm and intent. What had begun as playful seduction ended in a whirlwind of explosive sensation that left them both utterly drained and fulfilled.

Chapter 9

Over the next few days Andrew and Marina settled into what approached a pleasant routine. In the morning they rose early, had breakfast with Billy and planned an excursion for the afternoon. They went snorkeling, picnicked, tried fishing again, and generally enjoyed themselves. In the middle of the week they went over to St. John's for the day. Marina found the larger island fascinating, but she was still glad enough to leave after a few hours and return to Angle Key. Much as she tried to deny it, Andrew's home was rapidly becoming her own.

She was not unaware that with the attention of two adults who cared about him, Billy was blossoming. It wasn't that his father had failed him in any way, only that there were things she could give a child that he couldn't. A different kind of tenderness, a special sort of approval, in short, a mother's care.

She didn't want to think about that. For as long as

she could remember, she had wanted children. Whenever she thought of the joining and tried to imagine the man she would share it with, it was always with the idea in the back of her mind that ultimately, out of passion and beauty, there would come new life. But now she was discovering that she did not need to take an active part in the creation of a child in order to love it. Her heart reached out to Billy as surely as her spirit had, and he in turn responded with all the artless simplicity of innocence.

That was one kind of love. The other was no less powerful, but far more complex.

She was in love with Andrew. Try as she did to deny it, that stark fact burned in her mind. At home, very few people talked about love. It was something hidden, secret, even feared. She supposed that really wasn't so surprising. Even after so many generations, the struggle to survive had engendered a streak of conservatism that ordered human relationships and put the good of the society above all else.

Marriages were more often than not arranged between families for dynastic reasons. Oh, from time to time there were whispers that a particular couple felt rather more for each other than was expected. In fact, such phenomena were becoming less rare. But, still, it was something she hadn't really thought to experience.

Slowly, in learning about this new world, she was beginning to realize that it was a place where nothing was black or white, but only shades of gray. There was more violence on the nightly television news than she could have imagined encountering in her entire life. Yet there were also stories about people doing their utmost to make the world better, sometimes in groups, sometimes as individuals standing up to be counted.

That, more than anything, appealed to her: that individual men and women not only could make a difference but were admired for doing so. She realized that was not the case everywhere, but at least there were places where it was possible.

It was also evident to her that Andrew was making a difference through his work, though they didn't speak of it. She knew that he had given up the idea of her being a spy for a foreign government and had decided to trust her. The gift of his faith meant almost as much as that of his love would have.

At night, in his arms, she awakened to the full depth of her feelings for him and was almost brought to tears by it. He cherished her body so completely that there were times when she couldn't believe her feelings were unreturned. But there were other times when she would catch him looking at her in a way she couldn't fathom, and then she knew the anguish of doubt, and even despair.

Each hour that passed, each precious day and magnificent night, brought her closer to the time when she would have to leave.

Her repeated efforts to reach Theseus had failed. She could only assume that he was still being held in the Citadel. Their uncle, even if he had been so inclined, would not dare to endanger her brother's well-being, but the experience must still be terrifying. It was up to her to put an end to it. But first there was a task that demanded her attention.

"Do you remember," she asked one morning as they lingered over breakfast after Billy had gone off to play at a neighbor's house, "the ship we saw the first time we went fishing?"

"*Questor?*" Andrew asked. "What about it?"

"I was wondering if it's still in this area."

"Seems to be. When I was down at the harbor yesterday, somebody mentioned seeing it anchored about five miles out. Seems those crazy scientists are still looking for Atlantis."

"It might be fun," she said carefully, "to see how they're faring."

He shrugged. "If you'd like, though I suspect they may not be in the mood for company."

"Why's that?"

"They're probably tired of people saying they're crazy."

"If we do go," she asked with a smile, "I gather you'll be more diplomatic?"

"I guess I can manage that. Anyway, now that I think about it, the guy who looks after the *Sea Witch* for me mentioned that they had left some equipment with him to be repaired. He was going to run it out to them tomorrow. I'll give him a call and offer to take it instead."

"Good idea," she said, relieved by his ingenuity. She had been wondering how to get aboard the strange vessel and was glad to have the problem solved. So glad, in fact, that she didn't notice the carefully assessing look Andrew gave her as she cleared away the dishes.

The vessel called *Questor* rode at anchor in a calm sea. As the *Sea Witch* pulled up alongside, several people could be seen working on deck. Among them were a slender young woman with short blond curls and a tall man with dark red hair who, even from a distance, appeared to be arguing with her. His voice was raised and, as they drew closer, they could make out his words.

"Once and for all, Cassia, you aren't going down. The submersible is risky enough for anyone, but in your condition, you'd have to be nuts to get in it."

The woman, who Marina could now see was stunningly beautiful, patiently heard him out, then said, "You know perfectly well that Dr. Saunders said it was safe. Last time I checked, she was the one with the degree in obstetrics, not you."

The redheaded man scowled. He stood with his hands on his narrow hips, glaring at the woman, who looked back at him imperturbably. "Good for Saunders, but it doesn't happen to be her baby. I say you aren't going."

"And I say you're being ridiculously arbitrary. You know perfectly well that with Hank out with a broken arm, you can't manage the new modifications alone. You have to have someone along to help. Since I know the new systems backward and forward, I'm the logical choice. Besides," she added with a smile that bespoke her love for him, "Veda says you can't do it without me."

"Damn that snooty computer. The day is fast approaching when I'm going to wrench her chips out."

"That's no way to talk about someone—uh, something—who thinks the world of you."

"Must be the Wards," Andrew murmured as he maneuvered the boat closer to the boarding ladder. "Only married people fight like that."

Marina was inclined to agree, and had to admit to being intrigued by the pair. They weren't at all what she had imagined. She had expected to confront a couple of stuffy academicians, vague in both outlook and manner. Instead she thought she had never seen two more vitally alive people. Their personal relationship made them even more interesting, and it was with considerable anticipation that she looked forward to meeting them formally.

Their arrival had not gone unnoticed, despite the preoccupation of the project's leaders. A well-built man in his early forties with thinning gray hair and a pleasant, no-nonsense face raised a hand to them. "Ahoy, *Sea Witch*," he called. "What's your business here?"

"Equipment return," Andrew answered. "Ben Shagan's tied up, so we offered to drop off your auxiliary motor for him. It's working fine now."

"Come aboard," the man called, apparently convinced that their visit was legitimate. As they climbed up the rope ladder and stepped onto the deck, he came forward with a hand held out. "Name's Sean Garrison. I run the diving team. Appreciate you folks coming by."

"Nice to meet you. I'm Andrew Paxton, and this is Marina Lirularia. If you want to get a couple of your men together, we can hoist that motor up here."

Garrison nodded, his black eyes lingering on Marina with frank but inoffensive appreciation. "We'll take care of it. You had a hot day for this. How about a couple of cold ones?"

"Sounds good," Andrew agreed. He took Marina's arm, and they followed Garrison across the deck. Though all but covered with equipment, it could not have been more shipshape. "You've got some interesting stuff here," Andrew said. "Looks like you're into some pretty serious diving."

"You could say that," Garrison said noncommittally. He had brought them up to the tall, red-haired man, who was still in heated, though somewhat more muted, conversation with the young woman.

"Tristan," Garrison said, "these folks brought our motor back. Thought you might want to meet them."

"What…?" Distracted, the man turned to them. He was as tall as Andrew and well built, but that wasn't what struck Marina most. It was the keen mind she sensed in him, and the acute perceptiveness with which he surveyed them both in a single glance. "You're the physicist," he said to Andrew, "over at Angle Key."

It was Andrew's turn to frown. His profession wasn't exactly a secret, but neither did he care to have complete strangers aware of it. "How did you know that?"

"We've got a mutual friend, Simon York. He mentioned you worked out some equations for him when he was building the *Silver Zephyr*."

"Sure did," Andrew said, immediately more relaxed. He had only the fondest memories of his work with Simon York on the magnificent dirigible that had heralded the renaissance of stately, unhurried air travel. Any friend of Simon's had to be okay.

"This is my wife, Cassia," Tristan said, turning to the blond woman beside him. Like her husband, she was simply dressed in a white shirt and shorts, but in her case the shirt covered a belly gently ripened by pregnancy.

"It's nice to meet you," she said after Andrew had introduced Marina. The two women surveyed each other with an interest that didn't escape the men watching them.

"Thanks for returning the motor," Cassia was saying. "It's for the freezer. We've been getting by on dry ice, but that's been a hassle."

"I'm sure you've got enough to cope with as it is,"

Andrew offered. He was amused by his own reaction to Cassia Ward. While he was fully aware of her as a remarkably beautiful and desirable woman, there was nothing at all personal in that assessment. He might have been admiring a lovely statue for all the effect she had on him. That had nothing to do with the watchfulness of the man at her side. It was Marina and his all-encompassing feelings for her that made it impossible for him to want any other woman.

Tristan must have sensed that because he looked from one to the other of his guests with a faintly sardonic smile. "Either you're about the only two people in these parts who haven't heard what we're up to out here, or you're too polite to mention it. Which is it?"

"Neither," Andrew said promptly. "I was just waiting for an opportune moment to bring it up. Are you seriously looking for Atlantis?"

Cassia laughed softly. "Sounds crazy, doesn't it?"

Hearing his own thoughts so closely echoed took him somewhat aback. By the time he had recovered, Marina said, "Most people do think Atlantis is a fantasy, don't they?"

"Just about everyone believes that," Tristan agreed. "Even those who would like it to be real. But the fact is that there's been too much evidence of it over the centuries to be ignored. And now," he added with a glance at Cassia, "we've found actual proof."

"The newspapers said something about an artifact," Marina prompted.

Cassia nodded. "Would you like to see it?"

Surprised by the offer, which was far more than she had hoped for, she nodded quickly. With the Wards leading the way, they adjourned to the lab below deck. There, in a spacious, well-lit area, a table was laid out with fragments of pottery, several coins and what looked as though it might have been the arm of a small statue. Next to the table was another, on which a computer terminal sat. It was turned on, and a red light blinked at them as they entered.

"Hello, Cassia…Tristan," a female voice intoned. "I've finished the tide correlation. Would you care to examine it now?"

"In a few minutes, Veda," Cassia said. Seeing the startled looks on the faces of both Andrew and Marina, she laughed. "Don't worry, Veda has that effect on everyone. She's a bit more than your average computer."

"Or at least she thinks she is," Tristan murmured, though the look he sent the computer held a hint of affection. "Cassia was with the Center for Advanced Research before we were married," he explained. "She did the major work that led to the breakthrough in artificial intelligence."

"Of course," Andrew said. "I read your reports, but your name was Jones then, right?" At Cassia's nod, he continued, "I can't wait to get my hands on one of the new generation of computers. So this is the prototype for them." He looked at Veda with considerable interest.

"Prototype," the computer sniffed. "I'll have you know that when they made me, they broke the mold."

At his startled look, Cassia explained, "You'll have to forgive Veda. She has a very strong sense of identity, but we're still working on making her more courteous."

Another sniff, a few more blinks of the red light, and the computer was silent.

In the aftermath of that encounter, the items laid out

on the table looked almost tame by comparison. At least until Cassia picked one of them up carefully and held it out to Andrew and Marina for their examination. "We found this last year, when we were working off the coast of Bimini. The markings are a derivation of Minoan Linear A. Care to hear the translation?"

At their nods, she exchanged a smile with her husband and said, "It reads: Drink at Appesia's Tavern. We Have the Best Wine on Atlantis."

"Good lord!" Andrew exclaimed. "Are you sure? Not," he added hastily, "that I mean to question your ability, but if that's accurate, then how can anyone seriously doubt what you've found?"

"It's accurate," Cassia said with quiet certainty. "As to the doubters, I don't blame them for their skepticism. A discovery of this magnitude has to be carefully examined from every angle. The shard has been dated to approximately 2000 B.C., but that doesn't preclude the possibility that I could have added the writing myself."

While they were talking, Marina was staring at the fragment in fascination. She knew that she was looking at a piece of her own people's past, of which so very little remained that the tiniest morsel was considered precious. She couldn't help but envy the Wards their find, even as she dreaded where it would lead.

"You said you found this off Bimini," she said at length, thinking of a map she had noticed at the harbor. "That's hundreds of miles from here. What brings you so far afield?"

Tristan and Cassia exchanged a look before he said, "Because it's not all we found. When we returned for the second season, we were able to excavate a far larger area underwater. We turned up many more artifacts,

some of which you see here. One of them is a stone
tablet etched with what we believe is a map. It shows
very clearly that the entire Caribbean basin was once
above water, forming a single continent. Furthermore,
the map appears to indicate the location of several cities, including a major one that should be more or less
below right where we are now."

"I see.... So you're going to explore here?"

Cassia nodded. "We would have started already, except that one of our crewmen broke his arm, and our
submersible is out of action until he's replaced."

"My wife has some fool idea that she's going to
ride shotgun for me," Tristan said.

"That's an interesting way to put it," Andrew told
him. "It sounds as though you're expecting some kind
of trouble."

"Not really," Tristan acknowledged. "It's only
that—" He broke off, as though either unwilling or
unable to continue.

"Some strange things have been happening," Cassia
said. "Tristan hates to admit it, but it's true. There have
been blips on the sonar we can't explain, and last night
one of our crew thought he sighted a craft off to star-
board that didn't look like anything he'd ever seen before. It was moving very fast, but he did make out the
insignia of a trident on the side. It really shook him
up."

"Pete's always had an overactive imagination,"
Tristan said with a shrug. "Besides, it was almost dark,
so how well could he see, anyway? He probably spotted somebody's speedboat."

"He said it was fully enclosed," Cassia reminded
him gently. "With a large prow shaped like a dolphin's
snout that extended above the water. The hull glistened

like silver, and he could see lights inside, though he couldn't make out any people.''

''Doesn't sound like any boat I've seen,'' Andrew agreed. ''I wonder what it was.''

Marina didn't have to wonder; she knew. The description perfectly matched that of the small, fast crafts that were used for all manner of tasks outside the domes. It was one of those that she had taken on her journey, and which had been destroyed during the storm on the reefs surrounding Angle Key. Whoever had been on that craft had either, like her, taken it without permission or, more likely, been on a mission for the council. There was only one explanation that she could think of for such an effort: to discover whether she was still alive and, if she was, to bring her back.

She was struggling to come to terms with that when Andrew said, ''At any rate, it will be interesting to learn what you find down there.''

Cassia carefully replaced the shard. ''If we get really lucky, we may uncover the remains of a building or two. Of course, given the nature of what we believe happened here, there may not be that much left.''

''What do you think happened?'' Andrew asked.

''As near as we can figure out,'' Tristan said, ''sometime around 2000 B.C. this area was swept by a cataclysmic tsunami, a tidal wave. It could have been triggered by either an earthquake or a volcanic explosion. Whatever the cause, between that and the resulting tsunami, Atlantis was destroyed.''

''I thought Plato pegged Atlantis's destruction at ten thousand years or so before he was writing,'' Andrew said. ''Which would put it more like twelve thousand years ago.''

"You're right, but we think Plato was exaggerating to make up for how little he really knew about it. Also, there may have been some confusion in his mind between what happened here and events in the Mediterranean at about the same time that led to the destruction of the society we think founded Atlantis, namely the Minoans of Crete. Whatever the cause, we've got the shard dated to 2000 B.C., so we're sure we're on solid ground."

"Or water," Cassia said with a smile. "One of the reasons we picked to dive here is that the water's fairly shallow. But not too far away the bottom falls off into a deep trench that has never been properly explored. Sooner or later, we're going to have to do that."

And when they did, Marina thought, they would encounter something that would make their strange sighting of the night before seem as nothing in comparison.

Chapter 10

They stayed on board *Questor* for a short time longer, and before leaving they arranged to get together with the Wards later in the week for dinner. Tristan was clearly worried about Cassia working too hard and was glad of anything that might distract her. Marina understood his concern but, with one of those flashes of insight that came to her occasionally, she saw that their child would be born safely. It was a boy, though they didn't know that yet, who would be both as attractive and as brilliant as his parents.

"Nice couple," Andrew said as he steered the *Sea Witch* into her berth. "What do you think of that Atlantis business?"

"It...uh...certainly sounds as though they've done their research."

He nodded without looking at her. "I've got to admit, I'm taking it a lot more seriously than I ever thought I would. Those artifacts they found, the one

with the writing and the other one with the map, it's
hard to imagine what else they could be except genuine
remnants of Atlantis.''

''There doesn't seem to be any other explanation,''
she agreed. It was getting on toward evening, with a
light breeze blowing out of the west. When she had set
out that morning with Andrew, she had expected to
return to another evening similar to those they had already spent together. She would fix dinner, they would
have time with Billy, and then....

She broke away from thoughts too painful to pursue.
If life had taught her anything, it was that nothing was
ever guaranteed, particularly not the gift of time. However little of that she had expected to have with him,
it was turning out to be even less.

As they stepped off the boat, Marina averted her
head. Tears clogged her throat, and she was afraid that
at any moment she might break down. When he paused
to speak briefly with an acquaintance, she kept going,
not pausing until she reached the Jeep they had left in
the parking lot. She took several deep breaths and
dabbed surreptitiously at her eyes, grateful that there
was no one around to see her. By the time Andrew
joined her, she had managed to regain at least some
measure of composure.

''That was Ben Shagan I was talking with,'' he said
as he slipped in behind the wheel. ''It seems the crewman on *Questor* wasn't the only person to see that
strange boat. A couple of other people did, too. Their
descriptions tally with his.''

''Oh, really?''

Her attempt at disinterest did not discourage him.
''Ben thought enough of it to call a friend over in St.

PLAY BANGO!

AND GET THREE FREE GIFTS

It looks like BINGO, it plays like BINGO but it's FREE

HOW TO PLAY:

1. With a coin, scratch the Caller Card to reveal your 5 lucky numbers and see that they match your Bango Card. Then check the claim chart to discover what we have for you — 2 FREE BOOKS and a FREE GIFT — ALL YOURS, ALL FREE!

2. Send back the Bango card and you'll receive two brand-new Harlequin Medical Romance™ novels. These books have a cover price of $3.99 each in the U.S. and $4.50 each in Canada, but they are yours to keep absolutely free.

3. There's no catch. You're under no obligation to buy anything. We charge nothing — ZERO — for your first shipment. And you don't have to make any minimum number of purchases — not even one!

4. The fact is, thousands of readers enjoy receiving our books by mail from the Harlequin Reader Service®. They enjoy the convenience of home delivery…they like getting the best new novels at discount prices, BEFORE they're available in stores…and they love their *Heart to Heart* subscriber newsletter featuring author news, horoscopes, recipes, book reviews and much more!

5. We hope that after receiving your free books you'll want to remain a subscriber. But the choice is yours — to continue or cancel, any time at all! So why not take us up on our invitation, with no risk of any kind. You'll be glad you did!

YOURS FREE!
This exciting mystery gift is yours free when you play BANGO!

Visit us online at
www.eHarlequin.com

It's fun, and we're giving away
FREE GIFTS
to all players!

PLAY BANGO!

CALLER CARD

SCRATCH HERE!

YES!
Please send me the 2 free books and the gift for which I qualify! I understand that I am under no obligation to purchase any books as explained on the back of this card.

YOUR CARD ↘

BANGO

B	A	N	G	O
38	9	44	10	38
92	7	5	27	14
2	51	FREE	91	67
75	3	12	20	13
6	15	26	50	31

(H-MDB-OS-12/01)

CLAIM CHART!

Match 5 numbers	2 FREE BOOKS & A MYSTERY GIFT
Match 4 numbers	2 FREE BOOKS
Match 3 numbers	1 FREE BOOK

370 HDL DH2A   170 HDL DHZ9

NAME   (PLEASE PRINT CLEARLY)

ADDRESS

APT.#   CITY

STATE/PROV.   ZIP/POSTAL CODE

The Harlequin Reader Service®—Here's how it works:

Accepting your 2 free books and gift places you under no obligation to buy anything. You may keep the books and gift and return the shipping statement marked "cancel." If you do not cancel, about a month later we'll send you 4 additional novels and bill you just $3.34 each in the U.S., or $3.74 each in Canada, plus 25¢ shipping & handling per book and applicable taxes if any.* That's the complete price and — compared to cover prices of $3.99 each in the U.S. and $4.50 each in Canada — it's quite a bargain! You may cancel at any time, but if you choose to continue, every month we'll send you 4 more books, which you may either purchase at the discount price or return to us and cancel your subscription.

*Terms and prices subject to change without notice. Sales tax applicable in N.Y. Canadian residents will be charged applicable provincial taxes and GST.

BUSINESS REPLY MAIL
FIRST-CLASS MAIL   PERMIT NO. 717-003   BUFFALO, NY

POSTAGE WILL BE PAID BY ADDRESSEE

HARLEQUIN READER SERVICE
3010 WALDEN AVE
PO BOX 1867
BUFFALO NY 14240-9952

NO POSTAGE
NECESSARY
IF MAILED
IN THE
UNITED STATES

If offer card is missing write to: Harlequin Reader Service, 3010 Walden Ave., P.O. Box 1867, Buffalo, NY 14240-1867

John's and ask if anyone knew about it there. He came up dry.''

"There's bound to be some reasonable explanation.''

"Sure there is. What I'm wondering, though, is if maybe you could provide it.''

She turned quickly, her eyes widening. "Me? What are you talking about?''

He shrugged, as though the answer should be obvious. "It occurred to me that you might know what the crewman and the others saw.''

"Me? Of course not. That's crazy." All the more so because he seemed so calm about it. He might have been suggesting that she had some small, innocuous bit of information in which he wasn't very interested, but which she could reveal if she had nothing better to do.

"Like Atlantis?" he asked with a faintly mocking smile. "After what I saw and heard today, I'm not in so much of a hurry to dismiss any possibility. Including the one that says you know more about what's going on around here than you're telling.''

Marina laughed nervously. Her palms were suddenly damp; she wiped them on her pants legs, hoping that he wouldn't notice. The road had narrowed enough so that the upper branches of the plane trees framing it could meet and form a canopy that filtered the sun. Off to one side, a spring ran through deeply forged earth. She stared at it as they sped past, and struggled to gather her thoughts.

"Are we back to thinking I'm a spy?" she asked.

"If you are," he told her quite pleasantly, "you're not very good at it. Spies come equipped with elaborate cover stories and are trained to blend into their surroundings. What you have to say about yourself raises more questions than it answers, and as for blending in…the comparison is hardly apt, but a bull in a china shop would do a better job.''

"I presume," she murmured stiffly, "that you've thought about all this and come to some conclusions?"

He nodded, making a turn onto the road that led toward his house. "I've been removed from it for a long time, thank God, but I haven't forgotten what academic rivalries are like. They can get pretty vicious."

"Academic…? What are you talking about?"

For the first time since beginning the discussion, a note of impatience entered his voice. "Come on, Marina. You really aren't fooling anyone. Your accent, your interest in Greek history, even that absurd bit about not knowing who Socrates was, everything points to your being from Greece yourself."

"No, I'm not—"

"Don't bother denying it. Really, I have to admire your ingenuity. You get yourself onto Angle Key, find yourself a nice, safe place to stay and maneuver your way onto *Questor* with no eyebrows raised. Tell me something, did you know ahead of time that Tristan and I had a mutual friend, and that he'd be likely to trust me as a result, or was that just an added bonus?"

"I have no idea what you're talking ab—"

"I don't suppose you'd like to tell me what your real name is?" he went on relentlessly. "I'm not up on the current crop of ambitious archaeologists, so I probably won't recognize it, but I'm willing to bet Cassia and Tristan would." A short, hard laugh broke from him. "You know, it's really funny. Ever since I found you in my office, I've been worrying that it was my work you were after, but you were after something completely different, weren't you? What did you expect to find in there, anyway? Did you think I was giving Tristan a hand the same way I had Simon?''

''You seem to have all the answers already,'' she said quietly. ''So why should I bother trying to tell you anything?''

They had reached the house. He switched off the ignition and turned to face her. ''Because, sweet Marina, I'm going to wring the truth out of you whether you like it or not. Maybe you are off the hook as far as trying to steal defense secrets goes, but trying to steal anyone's work is despicable. If Cassia and Tristan do find the remains of Atlantis, it will be the major archaeological breakthrough of this or any other century, and they should get full credit for it. You're not going to get in the way of that, no matter what it takes to stop you.''

She made a sound somewhere between a laugh and a sob, but the tears gleaming in her eyes made her feelings clear. ''Believe me,'' she said brokenly, ''if Cassia and Tristan do find Atlantis, they're welcome to all the credit in the world. That is…if they live to collect it.''

Andrew froze. He stared at her in bewilderment for a long moment before his hand lashed out and closed over her arm. ''What the hell are you talking about?''

Numbly, she shook her head. ''You won't believe me. If I tell you the truth, you'll think I'm lying again, or that I really am crazy.''

''Try me.''

''It's getting late. You have to pick up Billy.''

He looked at his watch, saw that she was right and cursed. ''Tonight, after he's gone to sleep, we'll have this out. I can't believe you'd let Cassia and Tristan be in danger and not do anything about it.''

The contempt in his voice stung her unbearably. She stumbled out of the car and hurried into the house without daring to look back at him. Had she done so, her composure would have shattered completely. As it was, by the time she closed the front door behind her and leaned against it, she was blinded by tears.

The implacable necessity now facing her was almost more than she could endure. Her spirit rebelled, struggling against what could not be changed until she was left feeling as battered and bruised as if she had hurled herself against wave-pounded rocks. But then the courage that was such an integral part of her nature reasserted itself, and she saw through her pain that perhaps this abrupt end to all her hopes was actually merciful. To think was to suffer. It was better that she had time only to act.

Her thoughts suspended, she moved through the house and out through the patio door. Her feet carried her down the path to the beach without her being aware of their movement. When she reached the sand, she kicked her shoes off and left them where they lay. Moving to the edge of the water, she filled her lungs with the cool, sweet air. Before that breath left her, she had sent out the call she knew would not fail to bring a response.

After that, she had only to wait, but she could not bear to return to the house. Instead, she wandered farther down the beach until she came to the outcropping of rocks where she and Billy had stopped the other day. Trying not to think of him, or his father, she lowered herself onto the smooth stone and stared out over the sea.

Andrew returned from picking up Billy to find the house empty. In an effort not to alarm the little boy, he sent him to wash up and waited until he was gone before confirming what he suspected. The anger that flared through him when he realized that Marina was gone was nothing compared to his disappointment.

He couldn't believe that, after all they had shared, she would leave rather than tell him the truth. But even more than that, he could not accept her refusal to tell him what threatened the Wards. It was inconceivable to him that she would allow their lives to be in danger without attempting to help them.

So inconceivable, in fact, that he quickly dismissed that possibility. She would try to help them herself, and in the process become the target of whatever imperiled them.

"Daddy?"

The small, tentative voice of his son jerked him from his dark thoughts. "It's all right, Billy," he said quickly, putting a hand on his shoulder. "Listen, I have to go out for a few minutes. Will you be fine by yourself?"

Billy's lower lip trembled. He was, after all, only three. "Where's Marina?"

"I think she…uh…went for a walk and forgot about the time, so I'm going to find her." What he intended was to take a quick look on the beach. If she didn't turn up there, he would take Billy back to the neighbor, ask her to look after him briefly, and go out to the *Questor*. The Wards were somehow in the middle of what was happening, and he hadn't made the mistake of thinking he could solve it without them.

Billy agreed to sit down in front of the television set with a bowlful of Cheerios, his favorite snack. Andrew watched him for a moment before deciding that he was content enough to stay where he was, though probably not for long. He would have to hurry.

Long strides took him out of the house and down the path. The light was fading, but he could still see well enough to spot the shoes lying abandoned on the sand. Slowly he bent and picked them up, staring at them as though those mute objects could reveal whatever it was that they had witnessed.

For an instant a terrible fear gripped him. He had pushed Marina hard when he really had no idea of the pressures she was facing. Yet, he told himself in the next breath, she was a strong, sensible woman. Every instinct he possessed told him she would never do anything to harm herself.

Somewhat reassured, though not entirely, he dropped the shoes and continued down the beach. He saw the rocks before he saw her. If she hadn't moved, he still might not have noticed her. But she shifted slightly, drawing his attention, and he stopped, staring at her.

She looked…sad. It was an odd thought, since he couldn't make out her face, but there was something in the set of her shoulders that told him she was very unhappy. His anger at her was blotted out, replaced by concern. Before he could stop to wonder why, he hurried to her.

So lost was she in her thoughts that Marina didn't notice him until he was almost beside her. Then she jerked upright, her hands held out as though to ward him off.

"What do you want?"

"What the hell do you think?" he growled, his anger resurfacing as he thought of the worry she had caused him. "You were supposed to wait in the house."

"Was I?" She turned away, wishing that she could dismiss him from her mind as easily as from her sight.

"It's a nice evening. I decided to get some air."

"We've got a patio for that."

"Oh, for heaven's sake," she said abruptly. "Whatever you'd like to think, you can't keep me a prisoner. I'll come in when I'm ready, and not before." That last part was a lie; she never expected to set foot in his house again.

His big hands were clenched at his sides. She could see that he was holding on to his temper only with great difficulty. "We have to talk."

"Later." In desperation, aware of the swift passage of time, she added, "Where do you expect me to go, anyway? There's no way off this beach except along the path by the house. I couldn't get away from you if I wanted to."

"And you don't?"

"I—" One lie had been enough for her; she couldn't tell another. But she could choose her words with care. "If I could have what I want most, it would be to stay with you for as long as you wished."

Her stark honesty took him aback. He had never heard anything so unselfish, or so poignant. "As long as *I* wished? What about your own wishes?"

She shook her head sadly. "They're…unrealistic."

"Marina…" He took a step toward her, his hand held out. She knew that she should draw away, should say something—anything—that would send him back to the house. But she couldn't. Words failed her completely. She could only stand unmoving, her eyes wide and dark, as his fingers brushed over her arm.

"You are so soft…" he murmured thickly. "So warm and responsive." His pupils dilated as memory surged through him. "You were a virgin that first time, but your passion…" A crooked smile lifted the corners of his firm mouth. "You nearly drove me crazy, woman, do you know that?"

"It was mutual," she murmured, her eyes on the powerful chest concealed only by a single layer of sun-bleached cotton. His skin smelled of the sun, of salt air and of the faintly spicy soap he used. The scent of him had followed her into her dreams.

With a low moan, she touched him, gliding her hands over his muscled shoulders, down across the broad expanse of his torso to his narrow waist and hips. She felt his quickening heartbeat, the sharpness of his breath, the surging proof of his arousal.

His name was on her lips when his mouth closed on hers, his tongue plunging into her forcefully. He claimed her like a man starved for the sweetness she offered. His breath filled her; the taste of him drowned her other senses. She barely felt the arms holding her like iron bands, heedless for once of his strength. She was crushed against him, her breasts flattening against his chest and her sensitive nipples aching with their rigidness.

"There's nothing I would like better," he rasped when at last he raised his head and looked at her, "than to take you right now, here on the sand. I'd like to see you lying on it, naked, with that glorious skin of yours glowing."

His mouth returned to hers briefly, torturing them both. "I'd taste every inch of you, sweetheart, and then I'd be so deep inside you that you'd forget where you end and I begin. You'd forget everything except what we can do to each other."

Marina was trembling convulsively. The images he

evoked were so powerfully erotic that they threatened her very sanity. But for the slightest remnant of reason, she would have agreed to anything he wanted, let him pull her down onto the sand, strip her and take her without a thought to the total inappropriateness of such an action.

Only one thing stopped them, and Andrew acknowledged it with a wry smile. "But we can't leave Billy alone much longer. However, as you know, he goes to bed early."

He broke off, and she flushed wildly, envisioning even as he did how he intended to spend the night. "Andrew," she said desperately, fighting herself far more than him. "I need some time…alone, to think."

He frowned, clearly reluctant to leave her by herself for even a moment. "Why? What is there to think about? We obviously care a great deal about each other. Whatever else there is to concern ourselves with, we'll work it out."

What she would have given for even a fraction of his confidence, even born as it was of blissful ignorance. Managing a weak smile, she said, "Please, I know you don't understand, but I'll…be along in just a little while." Another lie, and this one took the last of her strength. If he had refused, she wouldn't have been able to resist him.

But instead he slowly let go of her and stepped back. His brow was creased, and the dark eyes watching her were unfathomable. Reluctantly he said, "All right. I'll see you at the house. But don't be long."

She nodded quickly, anxious only for him to be gone before she broke down completely. He had turned around and taken a few steps, enough so that she had

dared to breathe, when a sudden rush of sound from
the direction of the water drew his attention as well as
hers, and she knew with an abrupt sensation of horror
that she had let everything go for far too long.

Chapter 11

The craft rising above the foam-crested waves was unlike anything Andrew had ever seen. Even so, it wasn't completely unfamiliar to him. It perfectly matched the description Cassia had given of the strange vessel seen by the *Questor*'s crewman, and which Ben Shagan had confirmed was unknown in those waters.

Instinctively, he moved forward to get a better look at it, only to be stopped by Marina's hand on his arm. "Don't," she said urgently. "Get behind the rocks. They mustn't see you."

"You know who they are." It wasn't a question. He saw the truth in her eyes at the same time that he felt the pain stabbing through her. "Tell me," he said, his gaze locked on hers.

She shook her head. "I can't, and there's no time anyway. You must go *now*."

"No chance. What do you take me for, that you

think I'd be willing to hide and let you deal with this alone?''

"They won't hurt me," she insisted, trying without success to pull him back. He was as immovable as the rocks themselves. She might as well have hurled herself against them as to try to get him to do something he didn't want to do. *"Please…"* she sobbed, frantic to find some way to make him understand. "I'll be safe with them, but you…they'll kill you!"

"Why?" he demanded without the slightest hint of fear. "Who are they that they'd kill someone who hasn't done a thing to them?"

"It's what you could do," she said in a rush, looking over his shoulder and seeing the craft rising farther out of the water. In another moment the portal would be clear and the warriors would emerge. "It's a secret, don't you see? It has been for thousands of years. They'll kill to protect it."

He stared at her for a long, breathless instant as comprehension warred with incredulity. On a note of awe, he murmured, "Atlantis." Dazedly, he shook himself. "It can't be.…"

"It is," she blurted out. "That's where I'm from. Why I couldn't explain anything to you. It was against the law for me to come here. My uncle has undoubtedly ordered my arrest, but he won't actually dare to harm me. Someday…" Her composure broke; only with the greatest effort did she manage to regain it. "Someday I may even be able to tell my people what I've learned here. They might eventually decide that contact with you is desirable. That isn't impossible, only…"

"Only what?" he demanded, his voice as strained as the harshly drawn features that stared down at her.

"Only unlikely," she admitted on a thin thread of

sound. "We've been apart for so many generations that few of us even believe that the Outer World exists, much less that we should have anything to do with it."

"Not exist?" he repeated. "But how could they think..."

"There's no time," she all but shouted at him. "They'll see you. I can't—"

"Let them," he said harshly. "I'll be damned if I'll run from men who think they have to kill what they can't understand."

Marina gave up trying to argue. There was no time left. The craft was moving in toward the shallower water. Already the hinged portal that took up most of the front was opening and the landing ramp was sliding forward.

Without another word, she whirled around and ran from him. Her bare toes sent showers of sand flying behind her. Her heart pounded frantically. She could feel the painful tightness of her breathing, but did not slow down because of it. Her only thought was to distract the warriors sufficiently that they wouldn't notice Andrew.

A man stepped from the craft, with several others following swiftly behind him. They were all tall—or at least held themselves in such a way as to appear so—and broad-chested in the manner of warriors from time immemorial. Their plumed helmets of beaten bronze caught the fading sun and tossed it back defiantly. Beaked visors were pulled down over their faces, giving them the look of great hunting birds. Over their scarlet tunics they wore bronze breastplates fitted to every muscle and sinew. Their shins were covered with plated greaves. Each man carried a personal shield emblazoned with the insignia of his clan and his rank.

Double eagles were entwined on the leader's, marking him as a commander of the highest order. On what were still, for the sake of tradition, called sword belts, gleaming lasers shone.

Her uncle was taking no chances, Marina realized with a sinking sensation in the pit of her stomach. He had sent a body of crack troops to find her. They would not hesitate to follow their orders to the hilt.

The leader saw her first. He raised a hand gloved in mail and made a slight gesture. Two of the warriors detached themselves from the rest and jogged down the beach toward her. She made no attempt to flee from them, intending to offer not the slightest resistance. Therefore she was surprised that, as they came abreast of her, they drew their weapons. Still, she did not fear for herself, certain that the last thing they wanted to do was fire at her.

Andrew, however, didn't know that. Unfamiliar as he was with their technology, he recognized a weapon when he saw one. A low growl sounded in his throat as he sprinted past Marina and hurled himself at the nearest warrior, bringing him down with a flying tackle.

In her desperate flight to protect him, Marina hadn't even realized that he was following her. His sudden action stunned her. She stared in disbelief at the two men struggling on the sand.

The warrior was strong and well trained, but Andrew fought with the strength given only to men fighting to protect that which they love—be it an ideal, a homeland, or a woman. Though unarmed, he was doing a fair job of choking the life out of the man when the other warrior lifted his weapon and fired directly at him.

Marina screamed. Her very heart and soul seemed to have been rent from her. She dropped to her knees and reached out a shaking hand, drawing back for an instant as though in denial of what lay before her. Only with a long, shivering moan could she force herself to touch Andrew.

He lay unmoving, his arms and legs thrown out. All color had drained from his face. His eyes were closed, and already, it seemed to her, his flesh was growing cold.

''What have you done?'' she moaned, her gaze fixed on Andrew. Behind her, the warrior he had attacked straightened as his partner replaced his weapon.

''Come,'' one of them said, laying a hand on her arm.

She turned on him in a fury, her eyes blazing. Without pausing to think, she did something that never in her life would she have believed possible. In an instant of absolute, unbridled rage and pain so terrible that she could not bear it, all the considerable force of her highly trained mind was concentrated into a single, burning thought: to do to them what they had done to Andrew.

The warriors fell back, stunned by the force she unleashed. Not only was it immensely powerful in and of itself, but its impact was heightened by the total unexpectedness of her action. Even if they had known that she had such an ability, they certainly hadn't anticipated her using it, since the gifts of the mind were never turned to violence except for self-defense. That was a creed as old as the Inner World itself, but Marina was beyond caring what traditions she violated. All she could think of was Andrew lying unmoving before her, and of her own part in bringing him to such a fate.

So anguished was she that she made no attempt to follow up her attack on the warriors. They were able, with some effort, to recover themselves. Still shaking their heads in an effort to clear them, they approached her again.

"We must go," the older of the two said stiffly. "He will be brought."

Already another pair of warriors was approaching along the beach, carrying a stretcher between them.

"No," Marina said, trying to fight off their hold. "You have no right…"

That was meaningless to them and didn't even merit a reply. Her own strength vastly diminished, Marina had no choice but to suffer herself to be dragged down the beach. Looking back over her shoulder, she could see Andrew being laid on the stretcher.

"He isn't dead," the commander informed her when she was hauled up in front of him. He was a middle-aged man, his hair long since gone to gray, with strongly carved features etched deeply with lines. Even through the haze of her rage and pain, Marina recognized him.

"You have overstepped yourself, Commander Perseus," she said. "Above all, my uncle needs my co-operation. Now I can promise him that he will never get it."

The officer raised a thick eyebrow. "Because of the man?" He cast a mildly curious glance in Andrew's direction. "He isn't dead. The laser was set to stun. But," he added quickly as he took in the profound relief that tore through her when she realized his words were true, "I cannot guarantee his continued safety unless you do exactly as you are told."

Marina's joy was muted by the knowledge that she

was well and truly caught, but not even that could distract her from Andrew. She followed closely as he was carried up the ramp and into the craft. It was considerably larger than the one she had commandeered, but the basic design was the same. Beyond the control center were sleeping quarters for the crew and a small galley. Next to the latter was a cubicle which was customarily used for storage but which, she saw at a glance, had been speedily converted into a holding cell.

Still on the stretcher, Andrew was laid down next to her in the center of the floor. He was already beginning to stir, but he did not fully regain consciousness until the guards had left, securing the door behind them.

"Where…?" he murmured, sitting up with a hand to his head.

Quickly Marina put an arm around his shoulders to support him. Now that her panic had subsided, she could confirm for herself that he wasn't seriously injured. Nonetheless, she didn't underestimate the effect of the laser.

"Slowly," she said. "If you try to move too quickly, you'll get dizzy."

Either he didn't hear her or he ignored her advice, because he sat up abruptly, only to fall back. "Damn it," he muttered under his breath.

Marina didn't attempt to say anything more. She helped him to his feet and waited in patient silence until his head had cleared enough for him to fully take in his surroundings.

"This is the craft, isn't it?" he asked. "The one they saw from the *Questor*."

She nodded, knowing already what would occur to him next and dreading hearing him say it.

"Billy."

Marina swallowed against the tightness of her throat. There was such a wealth of anguish in that single word that she could hardly endure it. Softly, she said, "He's a very intelligent little boy. He'll know to get help."

"He's three years old, for God's sake."

She really didn't need to have that pointed out to her. Since coming on board the craft and being assured of Andrew's well-being, all she had been able to think of was Billy, alone in the house. How much time would pass before he realized that she and his father weren't coming back? Would he have the sense to pick up the phone and call the operator, as he had been taught? She could imagine it getting dark, Billy afraid and crying....

"We have to tell them," she said suddenly. Billy would undoubtedly prefer to be with his father, wherever that might be. The problem was that she couldn't be assured of Andrew's safety, despite Commander Perseus's implication that her cooperation would protect him. Caught between fears for Billy being left alone and dread of what he might witness if he was brought along, she was afraid to act, but she realized that there really was no choice.

Yet Andrew hesitated, if only for a split second. Holding her gaze with his, he said quietly, "If something happens to me, you'll look after him?"

Not trusting herself to speak, she nodded.

He waited no longer, but went to the locked door and pounded on it loudly.

A warrior answered and stood stone-faced as Andrew demanded, "I want to see whoever is in charge here."

"That would be me," Commander Perseus said. His fluent English surprised Marina. Only a handful of Atlantans were allowed access to the intercepted material that permitted such language study. She had been lucky to have had the privilege since childhood. Perseus had clearly come to it later in life, but had made a good job of it all the same.

He introduced himself to Andrew, who viewed him with both surprise and genuine curiosity. Marina had the impression that, under different circumstances, Andrew wouldn't have been at all upset by the adventure in which he was inadvertently caught. But the issue of Billy changed all that.

"I have a young son," he told the commander. "He's three years old, and he's alone in the house above the beach. He can't be left there."

Marina held her breath, fearing that the grizzled old warrior would dismiss a father's concern. But she was forgetting that Perseus belonged to a race that still lived with the threat of extinction, and as a result prized the life of every child.

Again he gave swift orders to his men. The portal had already been closed, but now it was reopened, and a party of warriors stepped quickly into formation.

"Let me go with them," Andrew said when he saw what the commander intended. "Otherwise he'll be frightened."

"I'm sorry," Perseus said, shaking his head, "but I can't permit that. However, I assure you that the boy will not be hurt."

Andrew had to be content with that, though he hated his powerlessness and despised the need to trust these dangerous strangers with the well-being of his child. Yet he had no choice.

After the cell door was again closed on them, he paced back and forth, his hands clenched into fists and his face an impenetrable mask that invited neither questions nor reassurances. Nonetheless, Marina felt compelled to offer what comfort she could.

"Perseus will keep his word," she said. "He's a decent man."

"Really? You could have fooled me. He leads a band of cutthroats and kidnappers. Very decent."

The whiplash of his voice made her wince, but she could hardly blame him. From his perspective, what he had said was true. "They could have killed you," she pointed out quietly, "but they didn't. I confess that surprised me."

"Am I supposed to be grateful for still being alive?" he demanded. "You know, that's a typical trap captives fall into, thanking their captors for the slightest mercy."

"I'm not suggesting you thank anyone," she said. "That would be absurd. All I'm saying is that the situation could be worse."

With a low sigh, he relented. "I know it could. Out there on the beach, when I saw them coming toward you, all I could think of was that you were in danger."

"I told you they wouldn't hurt me."

He gave her a wry smile and touched her face lightly. "Excuse me for not believing you, but when I see a bunch of guys who look as if they stepped straight out of the *Iliad*, I…"

"The what?"

"The *Iliad*. It's an epic poem about the Trojan War. You must have heard of it. No," he said, remembering suddenly. "You couldn't have."

"I'm afraid there are a great many things you know about that I don't."

He looked at her for a moment before he nodded

slowly. "I guess that works both ways. The Wards figured Atlantis must have sunk about four thousand years ago."

"They're right. In fact, their research and the theories they've developed to explain their findings are extremely accurate. If they continue on their present course, they stand a strong chance of finding not only extensive remains of what was once Atlantis, but also the present-day civilization."

"Which is why you said their lives are in danger," he murmured slowly.

She nodded, wishing desperately that she could refute him, but knowing that she couldn't.

Absorbed by the terrible problems they faced, they both fell silent and remained so for what seemed like a long time. In fact, it wasn't long before the cell door was thrown open again.

"Daddy!"

Instantly Billy was in his father's arms, held close against Andrew's strong chest as one big hand, trembling slightly, brushed over his tumbled hair. "Thank God you're all right," Andrew murmured hoarsely.

"Men came," Billy said matter-of-factly as he wiggled away from his father and smiled at Marina. He laughed at the memory. "Talked funny."

Andrew stifled a sigh. He was enormously relieved by his son's attitude—Billy seemed to think the whole thing was great fun—but when he thought of how many times he had warned him against going with strangers....

"When this is all over," he murmured under his breath to Marina, "that young gentleman and I are going to have a very serious talk."

She laughed, relieved that he wasn't so concerned

about the situation that he was unable to consider anything beyond it. But knowing that only made her all the more determined not to let him pay for her actions. Somehow she was going to make sure that he and Billy would be safe, whatever that cost her.

Beneath their feet, so subtle at first that they could barely detect it, powerful motors began to vibrate. "We're getting underway," she said. The craft had moved away from the shore but had not yet begun to submerge.

"Want to go see," Billy insisted, heading for the door.

"We can't, honey," Andrew said, catching up with him. He swung the little boy into his arms and lifted him high toward the ceiling. "Let's pretend we're flying instead."

Billy giggled uproariously. That was his favorite game, and he never tired of playing it. As she watched, Marina smiled wryly. It was a good thing Andrew was so strong, otherwise he would never have been able to keep up with his son.

They were still playing a few minutes later when Marina noticed that the vibration had stopped. She waited, expecting it to start up again. When it didn't, she said quietly, "Something's wrong."

He put Billy down and stood listening near the door. "I can hear voices, but I can't make out what they're saying."

"Let me try." Marina replaced him at the door, listened for a few moments, then said, "They're having engine trouble. Perseus has sent men below to try to repair it."

"We haven't submerged yet, have we?"

She shook her head. "No, and they're very worried

about that. The longer they stay above water, the more chance there is of being spotted.''

''Any idea how long it will take for them to fix the problem?''

Marina thought for a moment. ''No commander of Perseus's experience would undertake such a mission without carefully inspecting his craft first. So whatever's happened can't be anything major.''

Lowering his voice to keep from alarming Billy, who was playing quietly in a corner with a box he had found, Andrew said, ''I don't like the idea of our just sitting here. There ought to be something we can do.''

''You mean to try to get away?''

''Exactly. As long as we're still on the surface, we may as well take advantage of it.''

She bit her lower lip. ''It would be very dangerous.''

''But possible?''

He looked toward Billy. She could see the conflict warring in him: whether to place the child at risk, or accept a captivity which might lead to anything. Knowing him as she did, she suspected that his choice was a foregone conclusion.

''We have to try,'' he said finally. ''Otherwise there may never be any way back.'' Turning to her, he asked, ''Any ideas?''

She nodded slowly. ''I know the layout of this sort of craft pretty well, although the one I used was smaller. They're basically all of the same design, which happens to have been done by my brother.''

At the mention of Theseus, her eyes darkened. She would give almost anything to know how he was. But for the moment, at least, she could do nothing about his fate, whereas it just might be possible for her to help Andrew and Billy, as well as herself.

"There's a crawlspace," she said, "between the inner and outer walls. It can be reached through interior panels, and it connects to hatches leading outside."

"Sounds perfect, provided we can reach it from here."

"We can," she confirmed, if somewhat reluctantly.

The light of battle flared in his eyes. Marina suppressed a sigh. Men really weren't all that different, wherever they came from.

"Billy," he said, holding out a hand to his son, "we're going to have a little fun. Remember that movie we watched about the boys who found a tunnel under an old house and explored it?" The little boy nodded. "Well, we're going to do something like that here. We're going to play a little trick on the men who brought you. But we have to be very quiet or the trick won't work."

While he was explaining, Marina went to work on one of the wall panels. She found the latches that secured it and pressed them, causing the panel to pop out into her hands. The space this opened up was two feet high and about the same width. Beyond it lay darkness and the sound of the sea washing up against the craft.

"Are you sure about this?" Marina asked as Andrew bent over to peer into the crawlspace.

"Do you have an alternative, other than simply going along with your pals out there?"

"They aren't exactly my pals," she said, stung.

His face softened. "I'm sorry, that was uncalled-for. I realize you're just as angry as I am."

She was, though in her concern for him she hadn't let herself admit it. Anger would avail them nothing. It was far better, as he said, to use the unexpected break they had gotten to at least try to escape.

"Let me go first," she said. "I know the layout."

Andrew frowned. He wasn't comfortable with that, preferring to face any risks himself, but he saw the sense of what she was saying.

"All right. We'll put Billy in the middle."

"Come on, honey," Marina said to the little boy. "Let's see where this goes."

Carefully, she eased herself into the crawlspace. Light from the holding cell reached a short distance into it. She could make out the exterior panels. One of them, near where the passage curved around the hull of the craft, was equipped with a handle and hinges.

"I can see one of the hatches," she whispered over her shoulder. "It isn't far."

After taking a deep breath, she moved forward. She was aware of Billy following her. He was doing a good job of being quiet, as his father had instructed. After he had entered the passage, Andrew leaned back into the cell and fitted the panel back into place. Should anyone discover their absence, it wouldn't take very long to figure out where they had gone. But gaining even a few minutes might prove critical.

Marina had gone a few yards down the passage when she paused at the sound of voices. She could hear several crewmen speaking clearly, and quickly realized that she must be directly beside the control center. They were saying that the engine problem wasn't serious and would be repaired soon.

Spurred to even greater urgency, she sped up and, on her hands and knees, reached the hatch moments later. Theseus had intended it for use in an emergency if the regular portal was blocked or otherwise disabled. Instructions were clearly printed on it.

Before she attempted to turn the handle, Marina

pressed an ear to the metal plating and listened intently. She could hear water, which she expected, but what she couldn't judge was its depth. She knew that the beach off Angle Key sloped down quickly once the adjacent reefs were cleared. If they had gotten that far before being disabled, they were in for a tough swim. She had no doubt that they could make it, since they could easily tow Billy between them, but it would expose them to pursuit, or worse.

Still, there really was no choice. Praying that she hadn't misjudged the entire situation and would open the hatch only to discover that they were submerged after all, she glanced back through the dimness to Andrew. He met her eyes, correctly read her fear and gave her a quick smile.

The handle creaked when she turned it. The sound seemed to ricochet off the walls of the crawlspace. Wincing, Marina turned it the rest of the way and heard the lock click open. Placing her shoulder against the panel, she pushed.

A slit of light appeared. It was very faint, and only then did she remember that the day was all but over. If the sun hadn't already set, it would soon. Unable to decide whether darkness would help or hinder their escape, she accepted that it was too late to worry about and pushed the hatch the rest of the way open.

With a sigh of relief, she saw that they weren't far at all from the beach. Quickly she eased herself through the hatch and let herself slide into the water. It was cool, but she barely noticed.

Treading water, she turned and held out her arms to Billy, who had appeared in the open hatchway. "Come on, honey. It's okay."

His small face was pale as he took in the distance

from the hatch to the water, but, encouraged by his father behind him, he did as she said.

Billy landed with a splash in front of her. Though she knew he was a good swimmer, she quickly wrapped her arms around him and held him until she was sure he was treading water without difficulty. By that time Andrew was in the water with them and was looking around quickly.

"That way," he said, pointing in the direction of the beach. "The tide's going in; it'll help us along." As he spoke, he turned over on his back and slipped an arm around Billy. "Let's pretend we're in swimming safety class, okay?"

"Don't want to," Billy said stubbornly, trying to wiggle free. "Want to swim myself."

"I know you do," Andrew said gently, "but we have to hurry, so we have to do it this way."

The little boy's lower lip stuck out mutinously, and Marina feared he was going to refuse again. But after a moment the sense of obedience instilled by his father took over, and he did as he was told.

They struck out toward the beach, helped by the tide. Within minutes they had put a substantial distance between themselves and the craft. Marina was beginning to think that they would actually make it when a sudden shout alerted her to the fact that they were by no means safe yet.

Neither she nor Andrew wasted breath stating the obvious. Instead, they threw their energies into swimming faster. Even using only one arm as he was, Andrew had a smooth, powerful stroke. She had to concentrate all her energy on keeping up with him.

Over the pounding of the waves and the frantic beating of her own heart, Marina heard Perseus shouting out orders. They were out of range of the lasers, and his only other choice was to launch a pod after them.

Far smaller than the mother craft, smaller even than the one she had used, it held only two men. But that didn't reassure Marina. She knew that even with their head start, they couldn't hope to outdistance their pursuers.

Which meant that they would have to yield. Or fight.

"Take Billy and head for the beach," Andrew yelled as, without waiting for her agreement, he transferred the child to her. "The keys are in the Jeep. If you can reach it, they shouldn't be able to follow you."

Marina wanted to argue with him, but she knew he was right. She had no chance of holding the warriors off by herself while anyone else escaped, but the thought of what would happen to Andrew if he were recaptured....

"Go!" he shouted, swimming away from her toward the oncoming pod. The men on board saw him and swerved in his direction. Marina couldn't bear to look any longer. Tightening her grip on Billy, she struck out for the shore with all her strength.

Only when she heard the sudden shifting of the pod's engine did she realize, in a blinding flash, what both she and Andrew had forgotten, but their pursuers had remembered: she, not he, was their primary target.

Andrew shouted a warning, but it came too late. Even as she felt bottom beneath her feet, the pod pulled up alongside, and one of the warriors leaped in after her. Though she fought, she was powerless to keep him from wrenching Billy out of her arms and tossing the screaming child into the pod. He was about to do the same to her when a sudden yell from the beach stopped him.

"Hey," a man incongruously outfitted in a gray business suit called as he ran toward them, "what the hell are you doing? Let that woman alone."

The warrior didn't need to understand him to realize that he had been spotted. For a moment he hesitated; then, from the corner of his eye, he saw that the mother craft was submerging. Obeying the cardinal rule of secrecy, which overrode all else, he quickly reentered the pod.

Before Marina's horrified eyes, it sped away and swiftly disappeared beneath the waves, carrying Billy with it.

Chapter 12

"Let me see if I understand this," David Longfellow said. He was sitting in *Questor*'s galley, his jacket off and his shirt sleeves rolled up. Those adjustments in his appearance had changed him very little, in Marina's mind, from the pin-striped bureaucrat who had met them on the beach.

"You're telling me," Longfellow continued as he looked at Andrew, "that Billy has been kidnapped by Atlantans, as in men from the continent of Atlantis, which you say still exists somewhere under these waters. Furthermore," he added, shifting his attention to Marina, "you're supposedly an Atlantan yourself."

"That's it, David," Andrew said as he stood up and began pacing restlessly around the small area. "I always said you were a good detail man."

His sarcasm left the other man unmoved. With a slight shrug of his broad shoulders, he said, "You've got to admit it's pretty unbelievable."

"You saw the craft yourself," Andrew pointed out. "And you've heard what the Wards have to say about their discoveries."

Tristan and Cassia had shown only the mildest surprise when Andrew stormed on board their vessel, accompanied by Marina and Longfellow. They had listened to his rapid-fire explanation matter-of-factly, had wasted no time asking questions, and had given Marina merely the swiftest of glances before getting on about their business.

At the moment, they were both on deck, Tristan in the deckhouse guiding *Questor* to the spot Marina had identified above the undersea crevice, and Cassia preparing the submersible for action. If everything that could be done hadn't already been in the works, Andrew would never have stood for Longfellow's questions. As it was, Marina was glad to have him distracted, no matter how.

"About whatever it was I supposedly saw," Longfellow was saying. He was a tall, trimly built man, with light blond hair and a face that revealed little except what was made obvious by his very impenetrability. Marina knew men like him at home and understood that though they sometimes seemed slow-witted, that was often deliberately misleading. "You say it was a craft of some sort," he went on.

"What do you think it was?" Andrew asked shortly.

Longfellow shrugged. "Could have been any number of things—a boat, a seaplane, maybe even a weather balloon."

"For God's sake," Andrew muttered. "What does it take for you guys to own up to anything? Your eyesight's as good as mine, and you had a clear look at it."

"I was rather distracted at the time," Longfellow pointed out dryly, "by this lady here." He inclined his head toward Marina. "She appeared to be in some difficulty."

"And you thought the fellow who was after her looked normal?"

"Well...I will admit that the helmet he had on took me aback. But plenty of people dress in all sorts of getups these days."

"You're wasting your talent, Longfellow," Andrew said. "You shouldn't be in security. You'd be great as a government spokesman. Nobody would ever get you to admit a thing."

Longfellow gave him a swift, inscrutable look and shrugged again. He leaned back and looked down at the table on which their coffee cups rested. Marina's was untouched. Despite her recently developed taste for the beverage, she was certain that if she put anything in her stomach, she would regret it.

Over and over she told herself that Billy would not be harmed. But that didn't mean he wouldn't be terrified. Thinking of the child alone and afraid made her muscles tighten even more painfully. She stood up and walked over to the porthole. The last remnants of day had long since disappeared. The night was moonless, the darkness complete. Only by *Questor*'s powerful deck lights could she see how quickly they were moving.

"We're making good time," she said quietly. "With a little luck, we'll be over the trench well before dawn."

"But then we'll have to wait," Andrew said. "Cassia and Tristan are being a tremendous help, but they'd have to be crazy to take the submersible down before sunrise.''

Marina had to agree. While they would have to rely on the submersible's own illumination once they reached the trench itself, she doubted that she could pinpoint it without reference to the undersea landmarks that could not be seen at night. Much as she regretted the delay, it was unavoidable.

''You should try to rest,'' she told Andrew gently.

''There's no point.''

''Then at least let me fix you **something** to eat. You've had nothing since—''

He held up a hand, cutting her off. ''**Let it go**, Marina. There's nothing I want you to **do for me** except help get Billy back. Understand?''

Numbly, she nodded. He didn't have to spell it out for her. She knew that he blamed her for what had happened to his son, not only because she hadn't been able to keep the warriors from taking him, but because the whole situation was her fault. For all that she loved him, she had brought him nothing but trouble. Tears burned her eyes, and she blinked them away hurriedly, but not before Longfellow took note of them.

''So,'' he said, refilling his coffee mug, ''as long as we have some time to kill, how about telling me all about Atlantis?''

''I don't think that would be a good idea,'' Marina murmured.

''Why not?''

''Because most of my people don't want anything about us to be revealed. Besides, I don't think you would believe me.''

''You might be surprised,'' he said, choosing to

comment only on the second of her objections. "Why don't you give it a try?"

"Why don't you answer a few questions instead?" Andrew broke in. He wasn't sure why he was moved to protect Marina under the circumstances, but he couldn't seem to help himself. Resuming his seat at the table, he asked, "How did you happen to turn up on the beach when you did?"

"Coincidence?" Longfellow suggested.

"Try again."

The security man paused for a moment, then said, "Our last conversation worried me. I didn't like the idea of some unknown woman showing up on your doorstep, so I did a little checking."

"Using what? You didn't have any information on Marina."

"Not quite true. I had her name."

Andrew and Marina glanced at one another in bewilderment. With some reluctance, Longfellow explained. "You introduced her to several people on Angle Key. That's how I got it."

"Not so fast," Andrew said. "Are you telling me that one of my neighbors reports to you?"

"I wouldn't go that far...."

"How far would you go?"

"There's no point getting upset," Longfellow said, by no means oblivious to Andrew's growing anger. "You've got to see it from my perspective. I couldn't very well have one of our top scientists living on a remote island without having someone keeping an eye on him."

"Damn it," Andrew said tightly. "You knew one of the reasons I moved down here was for some privacy."

"And you got it, from just about everyone. But not from us."

"Who was it?"

Longfellow gave him a blank look. "Who was who?" Andrew started to stand up. "All right, all right. It was Ben Shagan, if you must know. He heard about Marina and passed the information along. He likes you, you know, and he didn't mind keeping an eye out for you."

"How kind of him," Andrew muttered. "I must remember to thank old Ben next time I see him. Thank him real well."

Longfellow grinned, rightly interpreting the method Andrew intended to use to express his gratitude. "Ben's a good guy. We go way back."

"I can just imagine the mayhem you've raised together."

"We've had our moments," Longfellow agreed. "At any rate, I ran a computer check on Miss Lirularia and came up blank." Turning to her, he went on. "You're an interesting woman. There's no social security number in your name, so there are also no bank accounts or tax returns. As far as I could find out, you've never applied for a credit card, driver's license, or passport. In this day and age, that means you effectively don't exist."

"You know all that," she said softly, "and you still don't believe us?"

"There could be any number of explanations," he countered.

"Such as?" Andrew demanded.

"Such as Marina Lirularia isn't her real name. That's the simplest one, but there are others. Maybe she isn't a U.S. resident."

"Bingo," Andrew murmured. "Who says you're slow?"

"Which is miles away from buying that crazy Atlantis story."

"I don't blame you," Marina said. When both men turned surprised eyes on her, she explained. "It is pretty wild, but the fact is, it doesn't matter whether you believe me or not." Longfellow raised his eyebrows, giving him an expression of surprised innocence no one should have been foolish enough to believe.

Marina didn't, but she still said, "You must have already realized that we're going on whether you believe what we've told you or not."

"Ah, yes," he said slowly. "The submersible. I suppose you're planning on leaving me here high and dry while you take off for the briny deep."

"If you're nice to us," Andrew told him, "we'll send you a postcard."

"From Atlantis?" he asked with a faint smile. "No thanks. I think I'd rather come along with you."

Their startled looks must have been comical, because Longfellow laughed. "Why so surprised?" he asked. "I admit there's only the slimmest chance that you're right, but what if it turns out that you are? You're going to need someone like me."

"I would be interested to hear," Andrew said quietly, "how you arrived at that conclusion."

"Simple. What you're talking about is making contact with a culture that to all intents and purposes might as well be on another planet. Right?"

"Not exactly," Andrew said. "But you're probably close."

"So you're going to need someone along whose report will be taken seriously by the powers-that-be."

Despite himself, Andrew laughed. "What makes you think you'll ever get a chance to report?"

Marina was wondering the same thing, but it didn't seem to bother Longfellow. "I've been in tight spots before. Nine times out of ten they work out okay."

"And the tenth time?" Marina asked softly.

Longfellow took a sip of his coffee and gave her a steady look. "When your number's up, it's up."

She didn't know whether he was really that unconcerned or merely wanted to appear that way, but in the final analysis it didn't matter. If he wanted to come along, she had no objections.

"It's fine with me," she said, "but the decision really rests with the Wards. After all, it's their submersible."

"And it's ready to go," Tristan said. He was standing at the galley entrance, looking from one to the other of them quizzically. "Is there a problem?"

"Not necessarily," Andrew said. "Longfellow here wants to come along."

"And who exactly are you, that you think you should go?" Tristan asked.

"I work for an agency of the United States government."

"I don't suppose you mean the Coast Guard?"

"No," Longfellow admitted. "I don't."

Tristan ran a hand through his thick red hair. "I don't much like the idea of what it is I think you do."

"You might change your mind about that."

"I don't think so. This is a scientific mission, not a covert operation."

"No argument from me on that," Longfellow assured him.

"Argument?" Cassia repeated as she stuck her head around the galley entrance. "What about?"

"About Longfellow coming along," her husband explained.

Cassia shrugged. "The submersible seats five, so there's room for him."

"Plenty of room," Tristan corrected, "since you aren't going."

Marina had been dreading this. She fully sympathized with Tristan's desire to keep his wife safe, but she also knew, as none of the rest did, that Cassia's presence could be absolutely vital.

Before the other woman could comment, she said softly, "Tristan, I know you aren't going to like hearing this, but if Cassia doesn't come, there's no reason for any of us to go."

"Why not?" he demanded, his brow furrowed.

"Because the odds of the submersible making it anywhere near Atlantis are virtually nil. We'll barely get into the trench before we'll be detected, and without Cassia to stop it, we'll be destroyed."

"I don't understand," Cassia said softly. "How can I possibly stop that?"

"Because you're pregnant," Marina told her gently. "I can get through to them and tell them that. Whether they believe me or not, they won't take the chance of killing a woman who's carrying a child."

"Why not?" Longfellow inquired, his professional curiosity aroused.

"Because," Marina explained patiently, "nothing is held more valuable in the Inner World than the promise of life. As I've told Andrew, it must be because we came so close to extinction that nothing is considered more important than children. That's why Billy won't be harmed, and why only Cassia can get us past the perimeter.''

"I still don't like it," Tristan said.

"It doesn't sound as though we have much choice," Cassia told him. "Besides, I'd already made up my mind that I was going."

He opened his mouth to tell her what he thought of that, then realized the futility of trying and shut it again. A moment later, he growled, "We know one thing about that kid of ours before he even arrives— he's stubborn.''

Cassia sent him a beatific smile, but said merely, "There's nothing we can do for several hours. It would be a good idea for us all to try to get some sleep."

Marina thought it highly unlikely that either she or Andrew would end up sleeping, but she nonetheless went along when they were shown to a small cabin. The Wards apparently took it for granted that their relationship was more than simply friendly, and she could hardly disabuse them of that notion. But it was very difficult to be with Andrew in such close quarters when she knew how angry he was at her.

Without a word, he sat down on the edge of the lower bunk and pulled his shoes off before lying back with his arms under his head and his eyes fixed on the underside of the bunk above him. For all his apparent notice, she might not have existed.

Or so she thought until a moment later when, without looking at her, he said, "Make yourself comfortable. We have to talk."

Although she had never seen such an arrangement of beds before, Marina was easily able to climb into the upper bunk. Though she had to be careful not to bump her head, she decided that she rather liked the idea, especially since she no longer had to look at Andrew's grim face.

"What about?" she asked when she was settled.

"Tell me about the men we're likely to encounter once we get there. What do they want? What's likely to get them to see things our way?"

"I'm not sure I understand.... I've already explained that the authorities want no contact with the Outer World; therefore, there really isn't anything you can do that will make them more amenable."

"There's always something," Andrew insisted flatly. "Unless human nature has changed completely where you come from, people are motivated by the same basic needs. There has to be a chink somewhere that will give us an edge."

Sadly, Marina shook her head. "I don't think so. My uncle, Orestes, who heads the council, has always been adamant about keeping Atlantis apart. He and his predecessors have made certain that few people even know for sure that the Outer World exists."

"So you mentioned. How have they managed that?"

"By controlling the information available to the public."

"So there's no equivalent there of free speech and free media?"

Marina had heard mention of such things during her brief stay. They surprised her, being what even she considered as very daring. "No, there's nothing like that. Atlantis is not a democracy."

"Then how is it governed?"

"By what I suppose you would call a ruling elite. Theoretically the position of councillor is hereditary, but new families have come in from time to time."

"Is there a king, some kind of monarchy?"

She shook her head. "No, we tried that a long time ago, and it only led to trouble. For centuries the most powerful person has been the head of the council."

"This guy Orestes. What makes him so afraid of the outside world?"

"I don't really know," Marina admitted. "It probably isn't anything specific, only a general desire to avoid change."

Andrew laughed shortly. "That's a pretty strange attitude for people who must have gone through the greatest change any of us has experienced."

"I suppose you're right, but that may be what made most of us so conservative. Safety became our primary concern."

"So that's what Orestes cares about the most."

Marina thought about that. Presently she said, "That and his own power."

"Good," Andrew said with a distinct note of satisfaction. "Now I know how to deal with him."

"How?"

"You'll find out soon enough." Abruptly he swung his legs over the side of the bunk and stood up. "I'm going to have a word with Longfellow."

He didn't ask her to come along, and Marina made no attempt to follow uninvited. Instead she lay in the bunk, feeling the vibrations of *Questor*'s powerful engines beneath her, and tried not to think of how little time they had left together.

Chapter 13

"Let's run over it one more time," Tristan said, "to make sure we all understand." He pointed to a chart spread out before him on the galley table. "We enter the trench here. There is a submerged mountain peak here." He moved his finger slightly northward. "Behind it, approximately a mile, are the caves, and beyond that we'll see the first of the domes."

"That's it," Marina said softly. "The mountain was the highest point on Atlantis before it sank. It's the place where the other group went."

"Those who refused to enter the caves?" Andrew asked.

"Yes, they thought it was mad to seek shelter underground, and they were convinced that those who did so would be drowned. They preferred to hope that the water would stop rising before the mountain was covered."

"I wonder what happened to them," Cassia murmured.

"It's impossible to ever know," Marina said. "But there were trees on the mountain, and they may have been able to construct a few boats. Perhaps some survived."

"I have to admit," Longfellow said, peering at the chart, "that I would have been pretty leery of going into a cave myself under those circumstances. That guy you said convinced most of those left alive to follow him there—what was his name? Theseus?"

Marina nodded. "The same as my brother. To this day, it's a very popular name in Atlantis."

"Yeah, well, he must have been one top-notch persuader. How did he figure it was worth the chance?"

"Because there was only one entrance to the caves," Marina said, "and Theseus believed that it could be sealed off enough to stop all but a trickle of water from entering."

"Makes sense," Longfellow acknowledged. "But even a trickle can drown you eventually. Besides, what happened when the air ran out?"

"Before it did, the pumps were in operation. They also held back the water. Construction on the first of the domes also began immediately. You must realize that Atlantis was already very advanced technologically compared to the other civilizations with which it traded. Partly that's because we reaped the benefit of contact with so many disparate people, but also, our land wasn't particularly easy to live on. We had to experiment and innovate in order to survive."

Quietly, her eyes filled with visions the others couldn't see, she said, "For the first few generations after the submergence, every man, woman and child worked tirelessly to hold the sea back and build the domes. Nothing else was done except to gather the bare minimum of food and purify enough air and water to live.''

''It's amazing that they were able even to do that,'' Cassia said. ''I can see how they would quickly have learned to harvest fish and seaweed, but the air and water…''

''That was the most critical need,'' Marina acknowledged. ''It had to be met before anything else could be done. Once again, Theseus found the answer. He discovered a way of purifying air by passing it through a porous rock that we know now has a very high oxygen content. He also developed a process for desalinating water using a particular type of lichen as a filter.''

''Oh?'' Longfellow said, his ears almost literally perking up. ''What kind is that?''

Marina gave him a steady look. ''I don't know the name of it in your language.''

''And you wouldn't tell me if you did. What's the matter? Having second thoughts about letting the cat out of the bag?''

Marina considered her grasp of English to be excellent, especially now that she'd had some practice conversing with native speakers. But the meaning of that particular colloquialism escaped her. ''What's that?'' she murmured.

''Never mind,'' Tristan answered. ''It's time to go.''

Out on deck, the early morning air was pleasantly cool. A brisk wind was blowing from the west, and a few high cirrus clouds streaked the sky. Marina looked around, thinking of how beautiful it all was. In only a matter of days she had completely adjusted to being in the open air amid space and sunlight. Home still called to her, but its voice had become muted. She took a last, deep breath and entered the submersible.

It was about the same size as the craft that had carried Perseus and his men, but was designed very differently. Most of the single cabin was taken up with equipment, most of which Marina couldn't identify. A large screen looked outward, and in front of it was the control console. Ranged behind that in a row of two seats, then three, was the crew's accommodation. She, Andrew and Longfellow took the seats in the second row, leaving the first to Tristan and Cassia.

"Be sure to strap yourselves in securely," Cassia said over her shoulder. "The ride can get a little bumpy."

Tristan flipped several switches, and a series of lights appeared on the console. Between them, he and Cassia ran down a long checklist. As they were doing so, she turned on a small computer monitor that connected Veda to the sub.

"About time," the computer murmured. "Let's get this show on the road."

"Instruct *Questor* to begin off-loading," Cassia said. "We'll descend at an initial speed of ten feet per minute, increasing to twenty-five at the usual rate unless countermanded."

"Last time he dropped us so hard my stomach stayed on deck," Tristan said with a grin. "But I think I've got the programming right now."

"'He'?" Marina repeated, bewildered.

"*Questor* isn't only the ship itself," Cassia explained. "It's also a pretty sophisticated computer that controls operations."

"Sophisticated?" Veda broke in. "Only if you think

white patent leather boots and miniskirts are sophisticated.''

''Are you suggesting,'' Tristan said evenly, ''that *Questor* isn't state-of-the-art?''

''Maybe by nineteenth-century standards,'' the computer muttered.

''There weren't any of you back then.''

''Hard to believe. How did you survive?''

''Not too badly, actually. It might be interesting to try it again.'' He cast a meaningful look at the terminal.

''Must we have this discussion now?'' Cassia inquired, doing her best to hide a smile, but not succeeding. ''I'm sure Veda didn't really mean to insult your work, Tristan. And,'' she added, ''I'm sure Tristan doesn't really think we'd be better off without computers.''

''Wanna bet?'' the two murmured simultaneously, only to break off in chagrin when each realized what the other had said.

''It's ridiculous,'' Tristan muttered. ''Arguing with a computer. Sometimes I think I'm losing my mind.''

''I can imagine,'' Marina said. She had observed the entire encounter with a combination of astonishment and fascination. Tentatively, unable to resist the temptation, she let her mind reach out toward the computer.

''What's that?'' Veda instantly demanded.

''What's what?'' Cassia asked. *Questor* had received his orders and was beginning to lift the sub so that it dangled above the deck at the end of the winch that would move it out over the water.

''I felt something,'' Veda insisted.

''We're getting underway.''

''No, it wasn't like that. It was…her.'' A red light on top of the terminal blinked furiously.

All eyes shifted to Marina, even as the sub continued to move. "What do you mean, Veda?" Cassia asked.

"She touched me."

"Don't be silly," Tristan said. "Marina is sitting behind us. She couldn't touch you without our seeing."

"Not like that. It was...I'm not sure." The little computer broke off, though the red light continued to blink.

"Do you have any idea what she's talking about?" Andrew asked.

Marina longed to say that she didn't, but intrinsic honesty prevented her. "I did touch her, in a manner of speaking," she admitted. "But only because I was so curious."

"But how could you...?" Cassia began, only to have her attention diverted when the sub touched the water. After submergence was safely underway, she continued. "I was wondering how you planned to contact your uncle and the others, since you said nothing about them having equipment capable of receiving messages from ours."

"That isn't necessary," Marina said slowly. She caught Longfellow's intent stare from the corner of her eye and glanced away. "Most Atlantans are telepathic to at least some degree."

In the aftermath of that bombshell, a pin could have been heard to drop in the sub's cabin. Even Veda was silent, though she was the first to recover.

"Fabulous! That's been the one big problem with humans. Getting information from them is so darn slow, but with telepathy..."

"Hold on," Andrew interjected. "Are you saying you can read minds?" A dark flush crept over his lean face as he considered what his would have revealed to her.

"Not exactly," she said, puzzled by his expression. He looked embarrassed and wary. It took her a moment to figure out why. She flushed and had to fight down a surge of anger at the mere thought that he would consider her capable of invading his mind without his knowledge or permission. With an effort, she reminded herself that he was an Outworlder, with a moral code that inevitably differed from her own.

"No Atlantan would ever seek to enter the mind of another unless that person knew exactly what was happening and had agreed to it. So far as we can determine, the skill developed in response to our extraordinary, life-threatening situation, and those are the only circumstances under which it is used: for the sole purpose of issuing a warning or asking for help."

Andrew was looking at her intently, all else momentarily forgotten. "That's what happened with Billy, isn't it?"

She nodded. "I called to him."

"He said it was his mother."

Marina's sea-green eyes widened. She'd had no inkling of that. "You don't think I pretended to be…"

"No, of course not," he said hurriedly. "But I do think he may have felt something in you."

"What?" she asked.

He hesitated, and she could almost see the mask slipping back into place. After a moment he said, "Never mind. What counts is that if you could reach him then, you can do it again now. Right?"

"I could, but…"

His mouth tightened ominously. The sub was picking up speed as it descended, but he barely noticed. "Surely you aren't refusing?"

"It's just that there's no immediate need, and without that, I can't justify what you're suggesting."

It was his turn to flush, but with anger, not embarrassment. "How the hell can you say that? We have no idea where he is, or what condition he's in."

So completely did she believe the guarantees she had given him about Billy's safety that she hadn't realized he was still worried. Worried about recovering him, yes. But not that he might actually have been harmed.

"He's fine," she assured him. "I'm not saying that simply because I want it to be true. If anything had happened, I would know it."

"How?" Andrew demanded, still far from convinced.

"I can't explain exactly, but if Billy were hurt, or even if he were very frightened, I would be able to feel it without having to reach out to him. I would simply know."

She fell silent, praying that he wouldn't press her too hard on exactly how she could sense Billy's condition. She didn't want to have to explain that such a connection was commonplace when an Atlantan loved someone. The minds of children, unlike those of adults, contained no walls for emotions to hide behind. Loving Billy as she did, she felt him with her always. But his father was a different matter. With him, her love brought no assurance of understanding, despite her wish that it could.

"The kid's got to be scared," Longfellow interjected. He was clearly suspicious of Marina's avowed ability, whereas the Wards seemed prepared to accept it.

"I have to agree with that," Tristan said. "Now that it's becoming more obvious that the Atlantans are very different from us, I'm beginning to be concerned myself about how we'll be received."

Marina cringed inwardly, wishing that he hadn't chosen to emphasize the differences between their two people.

"So far as Billy goes," she said quietly, "he's far too busy regarding this as a great adventure to be afraid. Besides, he's absolutely sure that his father will come for him." On a slightly ominous note, she added, "So is Perseus. That's how he intends to complete his mission, by luring both of us to Atlantis."

"He's succeeded, but I don't like anyone using my son as bait," Andrew murmured. The light in his eyes and the taut set of his body indicated that he was barely holding his anger in check.

Tristan shot him a quick, understanding look. "Hang in a while longer. We'll be there soon."

Andrew nodded curtly, but otherwise didn't comment. Marina could see that all his thoughts were concentrated on his son. She allowed herself a moment to consider what a good father he was, and how right it would be for him to have more children.

It was time to contact Orestes and warn him off before the sub could be spotted and attacked. Silently, conscious of Andrew and the others watching her, she began to withdraw into herself, following the path she had learned in childhood. Her awareness of her surroundings faded, until only Andrew continued to stand out sharp and clear. It was as though all her perceptions had narrowed down to him.

That wasn't right; she had to be able to block everything out if she was going to be able to make contact. For a moment she almost panicked, afraid that something had gone terribly wrong. But then a warm, comforting sensation flowed over her, steadying her breathing and soothing the rapid beating of her heart.

Her fear flowed away, her strength returned, and even as Andrew remained fully with her, she hurled her thoughts forward, straight and true as a warrior's lance.

Chapter 14

Orestes was angry. Waves of barely contained fury engulfed Marina. She was stunned by them; he had always appeared too rigorously self-contained to be capable of true rage. Belatedly she realized that he had merely been adroit at concealing it.

"You," he said coldly, "have violated the most fundamental of our laws. You have taken it upon yourself to jeopardize our security. You have usurped authority of which you are utterly unworthy, and in the process shamed both yourself and your family."

"I regret that I have displeased you," Marina replied with rigid courtesy. "However, the fact remains that the existence of Atlantis is now known to several Outworlders, including a representative of one of their governments. There is nothing to be gained by refusing to meet with them."

"But much to be gained by destroying all of you before you come any nearer."

"I have already explained, the other woman on board this craft is carrying a child."

"Why should I believe that?" Orestes demanded.

"Because not even you would dare to take the slightest chance of killing a woman in that condition."

There was silence for a moment, during which Marina could sense him struggling to refute that. Finally, even he had to admit that he couldn't.

"You will land at our private family dock," Orestes instructed her tautly. "And you will make no attempt to contact anyone else, otherwise nothing—understand me, Marina, *nothing*—will guarantee your safety."

"I understand," she murmured, "but I have one condition myself. You will have my brother and the child called Billy present when we arrive."

She could tell that he wanted to refuse her and swiftly backed up her demand with a nonverbal but nonetheless explicit sense of her own determination. Her uncle relented before it, albeit grudgingly.

"As you wish. Tell the Outworlders not to attempt to bring any weapons with them and, for all our sakes, try to give them some instruction in at least the rudiments of etiquette."

"They are not quite savages, Uncle," she told him. "Despite what you think."

He made no reply to that, but dissolved their connection, leaving Marina to return to her surroundings. Three faces peered at her anxiously; only Andrew appeared perfectly calm and in no way concerned. His ability to suppress his emotions frightened her, indicating as it did how thoroughly he was closing himself off from her.

"We can land," she told them, "but there will be

no official reception, and my uncle warned me that you are not to bring any weapons with you.''

Longfellow muttered something under his breath and began turning away. Andrew laid a hand on his arm, stopping him. ''Let's have it,'' he told the security man.

''I don't know what you're t—''

''The gun and whatever else you're carrying. Turn them over.''

''Hey, whose side are you on, anyway?''

''Ours,'' Andrew said. ''I don't want to see any of us get hurt, including you, and I've got a feeling that's exactly what will happen if we don't all do as the Atlantans say.''

With a grimace, Longfellow gave in. He removed a small, snub-nosed revolver from a shoulder holster and then, as Marina watched wide-eyed, lifted his right pants leg far enough to reveal a blade in a leather sheath attached to his calf. This, too, he laid on the chart table.

''You may regret this,'' he told Andrew, ''if things turn sour.''

''Maybe, but at least this way we've got a fighting chance that they won't.''

The security man continued to look doubtful, but the others turned their attention to what was passing beyond the porthole.

A dark shape loomed ahead, growing larger with each passing moment. She leaned forward, peering through the thick glass. ''There it is, Mount Prometheus.''

''That's its name?'' Cassia said with surprise. ''That must mean the Atlantans knew the legend of Prometheus.''

"What legend?" Marina asked. "It's historical fact that such a man existed. He helped to found the Minoan culture, which in turn founded ours."

"Amazing," Cassia murmured. "There's so much we can learn from you. Our knowledge of ancient history is riddled with gaps, whereas yours seems to have been preserved intact."

"Not really," Marina said. "There's a great deal that was lost when Atlantis sank. But you're right that whatever survived the submergence still remains. Our greatest material treasures are the remnants of our past."

"If only we have enough time," Cassia said. "If only—"

"Look," Tristan broke in, pointing. "That low ridge. That's where the caves are, aren't they?"

Marina nodded. She thought of the first trip she had made outside the domes as a child, traveling with her classmates. She would never forget the barely suppressed excitement she had felt as, safe within a craft much like Perseus's, they saw the ridge that figured so largely in their history. Later they were taken through one of the caves themselves and shown the cramped, dank chambers where their race had found sanctuary. Even the most boisterous of the children had fallen silent as they passed through what had become a shrine.

She leaned forward, her eyes straining against the dimness. The others sensed her excitement and made no attempt to contain their own. Even Longfellow's breathing increased perceptibly as the ridge slid beneath them and they moved deeper into the trench.

"What the…?" he muttered.

"Oh…" Cassia whispered in wonder. "Oh, my."

A series of lights had appeared before them, glistening like tiny stars. As the craft moved closer, the number of lights increased exponentially until what had appeared to be merely a scattering resembled a galaxy. Lights stationary and moving, lights golden and silver, lights large and small. Everywhere there was light that thrust the darkness of the sea aside and filled it with glittering majesty.

Soon the shape of the first dome could be seen, with the curves of others rising behind it. Within them stood proud towers linked by monorails, along which gleaming craft raced. Below them, between the towers, were swatches of green that looked like parks or farms, and reservoirs of pure, blue water.

Marina felt a sudden, fierce burst of pride. For all her disputes with her uncle and others, she could still acknowledge the great courage and skill of her people, and be glad of the opportunity to show it to others, especially to Andrew.

Instinctively, he reached out and put his hand over hers. Their eyes met. "It's beautiful," he said softly.

"Incredible," Tristan murmured. "I didn't imagine anything remotely like this."

"It's huge," Longfellow said rather more prosaically. "I was expecting sort of a…a lifeboat. But instead it…it—" He broke off, virtually stunned into speechlessness.

In the silence that descended on the small group, Marina said quietly, "It's existed for more than four thousand years. *Peaceful* years," she added. "We've suffered none of the setbacks you've experienced repeatedly in the Outer World, none of the waves of violence and destruction that periodically decimate your civilizations. Instead of having to constantly recover and rebuild, we've been able to progress steadily.''

''Bully for you,'' Longfellow muttered. ''But if I remember correctly, you indicated that there are plenty of weapons handy for when you people do start feeling violent.''

''That's unfortunately true,'' Marina admitted. ''But they won't be used against us.'' The group fell silent as Tristan maneuvered the sub closer to the first of the domes and then along its side. They traveled several miles in this fashion, with hardly a word said other than the occasional explanation as yet another wonder unfolded before them.

''This dome shelters the oldest of the cities,'' Marina explained at length. ''There is even a portion toward the center that dates from before the submergence. A temple to the Goddess Athene can still be seen there.''

''Does that mean the Atlantans still worship the ancient gods?'' Cassia asked.

Marina shook her head. ''In the aftermath of the submergence, there was an immense crisis of faith. People were convinced that the gods had failed them. A series of rather bizarre sects flourished for a while, but eventually a great prophet came who spoke of a single, loving God. It is said that the laws we follow today were received from Him. At any rate, today most people follow that faith.''

Cassia and the others were still taking that in when Marina said, ''Over there. Do you see the portal marked with the blue triangle in the circle?''

When Tristan nodded, she explained, ''That's the entrance to my family's dock. It's being opened for us.''

As they watched, the portal in the side of the dome opened. They passed through and found themselves in an air lock large enough to receive vehicles far larger than their own. Barely had the portal closed again than the water began to be pumped out. Within minutes they were clear. Ahead and above them was a second portal that, as they watched, opened to admit a small group of men dressed in tunics. At the center of them, his hand held securely by Perseus, was a wide-eyed, smiling Billy.

"Thank God," Andrew murmured softly. Forgetting her own pain, Marina touched his hand lightly. She, too, was greatly relieved to see the little boy again. He was the best indication they could have that Orestes was willing to behave sensibly. That conclusion was further supported by the young man who stood slightly behind the boy.

Marina felt her throat catch in the instant before a broad smile curved her mouth and lit her eyes. It was Theseus, looking none the worse for wear, despite his stay at the Citadel.

Andrew had sensed her excitement. At his curious look, she explained. "My brother. He was imprisoned for a short time to prevent him from helping me."

"It sounds as though your uncle plays hardball," Longfellow muttered.

Once again she didn't quite catch his meaning, but the sidelong glance he cast at the weapons still lying on the table gave her a clue. "Orestes has a long record of getting his own way. He is not a good man to cross."

"Yet you're doing so," Andrew pointed out quietly.

"Stubbornness," she told him, "must run in the family."

As they were talking, Tristan had unlocked the sub's hatch. "All set here," he said. His manner was calm, even relaxed. Only the faint pulse beating along his jaw revealed his intense excitement.

"If you don't mind," Marina said, "I think it would be a good idea if I went first."

"Of course," he agreed, and stepped aside to let her mount the ladder to the hatch. She eased herself through it and heard Billy give a yelp of pleasure.

"Marina!" the little boy exclaimed. "I knew you'd come." Despite Perseus's best efforts to keep him in check—which, to tell the truth, might not have been all that sincere—he wiggled free and raced toward the dock. By the time he reached it, Marina had stepped clear of the sub and been followed swiftly by Andrew, who bent and scooped his son into his arms.

"How're you doing, sport?" he asked with only a faint note of huskiness.

"Super! We had green stuff for dinner, and I got to play with a goat."

Amazed that such events would have pleased his son so greatly, Andrew was left faintly bemused. But that was inconsequential when compared to his overwhelming relief. Though he was well aware that the danger was far from over, now he at least had some hope of a less-than-disastrous conclusion to the affair.

"You've had quite an adventure," he told his son as he set him back on his feet. "I want you to tell me all about it, but first we have to meet these people."

Billy nodded and, tugging on his father's hand, led him forward. But it was Marina who made the introductions after the others had emerged from the sub. There was no opportunity for a private word with Theseus, but brother and sister did manage to exchange a loving smile. Andrew noted that the young man had ebony hair similar to Marina's, but that his eyes were blue and his features less delicate. He didn't miss the quick, assessing look Theseus shot him, a glance that held a world of questions and the clear intention to get the answers. That was an encounter Andrew was looking forward to, but first he had to get past Orestes and his colleagues.

"You must understand," Marina's uncle said stiffly to the party in general, "that your presence was uninvited; therefore we cannot regard you as guests." He was a tall, distinguished-looking man of middle years, with gray hair, piercing blue eyes and chiseled features. He held himself with the erectness of an old warrior who, though past his prime, still remembered the skills of his craft. His manner was overwhelmingly patrician, even in the way he carried one end of his cloak folded over his arm. He spoke in slightly accented English, which saved Marina the trouble of translating.

"Don't worry about it," Longfellow assured him. "We're not here to enjoy ourselves. By the way, I'm a representative of the United States government. Our President sends you greetings."

Since the gentleman in question was in blissful ignorance of how his name was being used, Marina thought the security man was going a bit far. But Longfellow was only getting wound up. "Naturally," he continued, "we'll want to start laying the groundwork for an exchange of delegations. I'm sure you'll agree that we have many points of mutual interest to be discussed."

Orestes gave him a look that strongly suggested he had found something nasty on the sole of his sandal. "There is only one point," he said flatly. "How to repair the damage done by my niece's irresponsible behavior. Marina, you will attend me in council immediately. The others will be held in appropriate quarters until a decision is reached.''

"Hold on," Andrew said. "Marina isn't going anywhere by herself. Not, that is, if you want us to cooperate in keeping our presence here a secret."

Orestes's brow furrowed. The look he turned on Andrew had undoubtedly shriveled many a lesser man. Andrew ignored it. He was already taking the measure of Marina's uncle, deciding that while he appeared intelligent enough, and perhaps even sensible, he was also afraid. Like many people in such a state, he was attempting to compensate for it by bullying.

"You are in no position to be making demands, Dr. Paxton," Orestes said. "Must I remind you that you are here only at my sufferance, which could be withdrawn at any time?"

"Hey," Longfellow interjected, "there's no reason for anyone to be getting upset." Under his breath, he muttered, "Leave this to me. You're going to blow the whole thing."

"I don't think so," Andrew said, addressing Orestes as much as the security man. "Our hosts have a vested interest in keeping us alive and well, if only to find out how much information about Atlantis has become known outside."

"You mean there are others who know?" Orestes began, turning an accusing stare on Marina.

"Our mother ship contains a large crew," Tristan broke in, exaggerating only slightly. "They are aware of our location. If we haven't returned within a suitable length of time, they will take the appropriate steps."

Longfellow nodded approvingly, but also felt called upon to add, "And there's no sense thinking about putting them out of the way. Washington is fully aware of our movements.'' This was a complete bluff, since he hadn't even considered notifying his superiors, who would undoubtedly have labeled him a flake and begun processing his retirement papers. But Orestes had no way of knowing that.

The half dozen or so other councillors who were ranked behind Orestes muttered among themselves and shook their heads. They were all older men who had expected to pass on long before anything intruded on the peace and security they had known all their lives. Now it appeared that such was not to be the case.

''Very well,'' Orestes said from between tightly compressed lips. ''You will all come along to the council chamber. We will hear what you have to say, but I make no promises.''

On that note of warning they left the dock and boarded a swiftly running silver vehicle that carried them deeper into the heart of the city. At the end of perhaps a two-mile ride, they disembarked before a low, stone building set in what appeared to be a small private park.

The two-story structure was gracefully elegant without being in the least pretentious. Andrew privately thought that any people who would have such a place as their seat of government couldn't possibly be all bad. He considered the bureaucratic excesses that were regular fodder on the nightly news and wondered if it might be possible to export the Atlantans' innate sense of dignity. Even the far larger towers he could see in the distance appeared in keeping with their surroundings, rather than imposed on them.

''Something I don't understand,'' he murmured to Marina. ''We can see perfectly, and it's pleasantly warm, yet sunlight can't possibly penetrate this far. What accounts for it?"

Though he had spoken softly, Orestes overheard him. He turned as they entered the building and said with unmistakable firmness, "I forbid you to answer that, Marina. You will reveal nothing more about us than you have said already."

"But Uncle," Theseus broke in, "there could hardly be any harm in explaining our source of energy. After all…"

"Enough," the high councillor ordered, raising a peremptory hand. He had caught the avid gleam in Longfellow's eyes and, though he didn't fully know what accounted for it, he sensed that here was an advantage to be gained. "In time perhaps it will be explained, but not before a great many other matters are worked out first."

"Talk about waving the carrot in front of the donkey," Tristan murmured. "If these people have worked out a simple, efficient source of energy that doesn't pollute…"

"Which they must have, in order to survive this long and build on the scale they have," Cassia said. Like her husband, she had said little but missed nothing. Though she could still barely believe where they were, she was taking in every detail with rapt attention.

The council chamber was in keeping with the building that housed it. A long, high-ceilinged room, it was furnished at one end with a raised platform positioned in front of a fresco depicting the domes as seen from outside. A school of dolphins swam past, appearing to pause and admire the city. Nearby figures of men and women, their faces obscured by breathing apparatus, could be seen going about various tasks.

"It's astonishing how well you've adapted," Andrew said sincerely. "No one would have believed it possible for people to be so at home in the sea."

"It was a great challenge," Orestes admitted grudgingly. "Thankfully, our ancestors rose to the occasion."

"I would say they did rather more than that. Our people are taking the first steps into space with the hope that we may eventually be able to establish colonies there. But we're very far from achieving anything similar to this."

Despite himself, Orestes preened slightly. Marina hid a smile. She knew her uncle must be telling himself that the Outworlders couldn't be all bad if they had the sense to recognize superiority when they saw it. The mention of space, though, gave him pause.

"Does that mean," he ventured after the councillors had taken their seats before the fresco, leaving their visitors standing facing them, "that you intend to leave this planet?"

"You mean all of us?" Andrew asked, somewhat taken aback by the notion. But the Atlantans appeared to be seriously entertaining it, which prompted him to explain. "A small number of us may go eventually, when it's possible, but certainly the vast majority would stay here. This is, after all, a beautiful world."

Orestes thought that over. His face took on an uncompromisingly stern look. "Then why," he demanded, "are you so eager to destroy it?"

Andrew and Tristan exchanged a quick glance, while behind them Longfellow scowled. "Where did you get that idea?" he asked.

"Do you take us for fools? Since we first became aware that the entire world had not been engulfed by the deluge as we initially thought, we have taken care to watch you. Your behavior has appalled us. You have gone from bad to worse, with destruction your only apparent goal. That is why we have been so scrupulous to avoid all contact with you, and even to shelter most of our people from the knowledge of your very existence.''

''I'll admit we've had some problems....'' Andrew said.

''Problems? I speak as one proud to have served as a warrior for most of my adult life. I have stood ever ready to defend Atlantis, and I have never shied from the thought of violence should it be necessary, but I tell you this: never would any Atlantan engage in wanton destruction for its own sake, and that is what you Outworlders have done again and again. It's as though you despise life itself and seek every opportunity to end it.''

''That isn't true,'' Cassia protested. ''Andrew is right; there are problems. But we're dealing with them. None of us wants to see the world destroyed.'' Unconsciously, she touched a hand softly to her belly. ''We want to keep it safe for our children and make their lives better than our own.''

Orestes's face softened slightly, though he continued to look at them disapprovingly. ''So you say, but your actions contradict your words. You are a dangerous people, and I cannot countenance risking our own contamination through contact with you.''

''It doesn't appear that you have much choice,'' Andrew said quietly. ''After all, we *are* here.''

The high councillor nodded. He glanced toward Perseus, who, with his men, had accompanied them from the dock. ''That is irrefutable,'' Orestes said. ''However, only if you are permitted to go free will there be difficulties. That I cannot allow.''

''I told you,'' Tristan broke in, ''our crew is aware of where we've gone.''

''And they will shortly be joining you in your extended stay here.'' He raised a hand, and Perseus instantly obeyed. The warrior left the chamber smartly, taking several of his men with him.

''The craft you arrived in,'' Orestes said, ''appears quite simple.'' He ignored Tristan's raised eyebrows and continued. ''It will not take very long for us to understand its operation. Perseus and a party of warriors will return to your vessel, take it over and transfer the crew here. Your craft will be found floating derelict, the fate of those on board it never to be known.''

''Sounds like they've pulled this before,'' Andrew murmured, thinking of the many mysterious disappearances that had occurred over the centuries in the waters of the Caribbean.

''As to the possibility that your government has been informed,'' Orestes continued, looking directly at Longfellow, ''we will simply have to take the chance that such is not the case.'' His expression made it clear that he hadn't believed the security man for a moment. ''Naturally, you will not be allowed to mingle freely with the population; however, your every comfort will be seen to. You will have ample opportunity to follow those pursuits that interest you. In time you may even come to accept your fate. I hope so,'' he concluded. ''For, whether you do or not, none of you will see home again.''

Chapter 15

"I'm so sorry," Marina said. She and Andrew were sitting in a small garden that adjoined the quarters they had been assigned. The villa was on a secluded hillside overlooking the city. It stood behind high stone walls, which were patrolled at regular intervals by an elite squadron of guards.

"When I began all this," she went on quietly, "I had no idea it would work out this way."

"I understand," Andrew said. His lack of anger surprised her. Since the meeting in the council chamber he had been largely silent, preoccupied with his own thoughts. Throughout the simple meal they had shared, he had said little. Billy had done most of the talking, regaling them with the details of his adventure. But eventually the excitement of the day had caught up with him, and he had fallen asleep.

Marina had hoped that, while he napped, she and Andrew might come to some accord. Though she deeply regretted his captivity, she couldn't help but be intensely glad that they were together. However, she fully realized that their proximity didn't mean their relationship was to continue as it had been.

"Perhaps," she murmured, "my uncle will eventually reconsider and allow you to leave."

"I don't think so. He seems pretty set in his ways."

"It's so unfair."

He made a small, dismissive gesture. "The guy who was my commander in Vietnam used to say that 'fair' had only one meaning: a place with rides and carny booths."

Marina gathered that he wasn't surprised by Orestes's actions. Seeking anything that might change the subject, she asked, "What's Vietnam?"

Andrew sighed. "A war we fought awhile ago. It didn't work out too well."

"Have any of them?"

He shrugged. "The ones that have preserved freedom, which is just a way of saying human dignity."

"We have a degree of freedom here," Marina said quietly, "including freedom from war, but sometimes I wonder if our government shouldn't trust its own people more."

"You mean with something like information about the Outer World?"

She nodded. "That's right. I've come to believe that if the people were given all the available information and asked to make a decision about whether or not they wanted contact, they would say that they did."

"But Orestes doesn't want them to have that choice?"

"As he said, he's afraid of contamination."

Andrew didn't respond. He had lapsed back into si-

lence and sat staring off into the middle distance. A
light breeze, the product of the giant ventilation fans
that turned constantly in the tunnels beneath the city,
ruffled the leaves of a pear tree. Marina gazed at it,
seeing the ripening fruit glowing golden in the trans-
lucent light. She breathed in the scents of living things,
things of the earth lovingly nurtured through the centuries, reminders of an existence that had been preserved against all odds.

Atlantans, she thought, did not give up easily. To
anyone familiar with their history, that ought to appear
self-evident, but it had only just occurred to her. It
might be said that stubbornness was a quality her people had in abundance. Her feelings of defeat shamed
her heritage, yet she could not shake them. Rarely in
her life had she felt so overwhelmed by circumstances
as to be unable to think of any action that might improve them. When she did, she knew that the only
course that helped at all was to get away by herself.

"I'm a bit grimy," she said. "I think I'll get cleaned
up."

He nodded, but seemed to barely notice her departure. In her room, she removed the clothes she had put
on the previous day, wondering when, if ever, she
would wear them again. They were a part of a world
she had left behind and to which she could have no
expectation of ever returning. Orestes would see to
that. But thoughts of her uncle would only lead her
further into futile anger. To avoid that, she resolutely
turned her attention to a hot bath.

Water used for that purpose came from a different
source than the supplies kept for drinking and cooking.
It wasn't completely desalinated, and the remaining
salts gave it a pleasantly reviving effect. After soaking

for half an hour, Marina felt better able to face whatever lay ahead.

She had risen gracefully from the sunken tub and was reaching for a towel when she suddenly became aware that she was not alone. Andrew had entered the room soundlessly. He stood looking at her, his face in shadows, inscrutable. She parted her lips to speak, but no words came. There were none to express the conflict of hope and fear whirling through her.

How foolish to want to be with him one last time when that could only make the hurt worse and draw it out longer. Yet how irresistible the temptation.

He took a step toward her. She was aware of his eyes taking in her nudity and saw the tremor in the hand he raised. His fingers brushed her with aching gentleness, barely touching the silken cascade of hair she had piled on top of her head. Slowly, he removed the ivory pins that held it, taking them out one by one, so that the gleaming strands fell across her shoulders and breasts, gradually hiding her from his gaze.

When the last of the pins was gone, he laid them on a nearby marble table, then turned back to study her with reverent intensity. "I imagine," he murmured huskily, "that Aphrodite rising from the waves must have looked as you do."

She made a tiny gesture of denial, which he quickly quashed. "You must know how beautiful you are. Ever since I saw you for the first time, I've been unable to even imagine a lovelier woman. It isn't only how you look. There's something inside...." A short, self-deprecating laugh broke from him. "Don't misunderstand me. The way you look is responsible for quite a bit of what I'm feeling right now."

Desire. She told herself that was all he meant, and

the knowledge hurt her. Her throat tightened, and she moved to turn away from him.

"Don't," he said, his voice suddenly soft and almost entreating. "It's impossible even to be sure of what the next few hours will hold, but at least we have this moment. Let's make the most of it."

She wanted to ask him what he meant, what he thought might happen so soon. But his mouth closed over hers before she could speak, and she was lost in the whirlwind of sensations he provoked.

With her still-damp body crushed against his, his arm an iron band around her narrow waist and his big hand cupping her buttocks, it was impossible for her to move. Yet, oddly, she felt no sense of confinement. Her spirit soared above all regret and sadness. As he had said, they had the moment.

Brief though it was, it seemed to stretch into an eternity. There was no hurry in his movements as he lifted her into his arms and carried her to the large bed curtained in gauze.

She wasn't sure what happened to his clothes. They were there, and then they weren't. His skin felt very hot, as hers had when it was burned by the sun, as it did now when burned by a fire of a very different sort.

By contrast, his tongue felt cool on her nipples. He suckled her for what seemed like a very long time, first one, then the other. The deep ripples his attention brought to her womb made her cry out. Her fingers tangled in his thick hair as she tried to pull his head up. He resisted, continuing his sweet torture, until her hands fell away and she lay drowning in pleasure beneath him.

When her breasts were so exquisitely sensitized that she could hardly bear even the touch of the air on them, he moved farther down her body. Dimly she sensed the urgency in him and marveled at how he could restrain it. All his strength and skill were focused strictly on her. He explored her inch by inch, tasting and caressing until she thought she would go mad from the floodtide of sensation exploding within her.

She cried out, the sound reverberating in her mind. There had to be an end; it could not go on forever. When his hands parted her thighs, his callused thumbs rubbing against her silken inner skin, she made no attempt to resist him.

"Beautiful," he muttered thickly before his mouth touched her. So ready was she that the slightest flick of his tongue brought her to a shattering peak. For several moments she was aware of nothing except being lifted out of her body and hurled into another universe in which only the two of them existed.

He let her descend slowly, holding her against the taut length of his body, his hands stroking her back soothingly. When she had recovered sufficiently to realize what was happening, she looked at him in bewilderment. "You didn't…"

He shook his head, smiling faintly. "Not yet, but soon." Then he was within her, brought there by a single, powerful thrust that left them both gasping. How perfectly they fit together, as though made for no other purpose than this union. So transcendent was the sensation that neither felt the need to do more until, of its own volition, her body tightened around him.

A low groan broke from him. He moved with supreme skill to wring a cry of ecstasy from her, quickly followed by his own. Her back arched as her hands and arms clasped him ever closer. Together they found the ultimate in fulfillment before falling exhausted into sleep, their bodies still intimately entwined.

Marina was alone when she awoke. She returned to consciousness as abruptly as she had left it, her eyelids flying open. The memory of what had passed between them stunned her. She didn't know whether to wish she had simply imagined it, or to be glad it had actually happened.

Her body, however, had ideas of its own. She practically purred with contentment as she left the bed and swiftly began to dress. At least, she tried to hurry, despite the fact that all her movements were imbued with a sweet languor she could not shake. Nor could she banish the purely female smile that haunted her mouth and eyes. The woman she glimpsed in the mirror looked eminently satisfied, yet undeniably worried, which described her perfectly.

Without surprise, she found that a cedar chest near the bed held part of her own wardrobe. Orestes was, if nothing else, known for his meticulousness.

Dressed in a pleated, ankle-length tunic secured by a belt of gold studded with lapis lazuli, she sat before a mirror to brush her hair. When that was done she looked at herself critically. Anyone with half an ounce of sense, seeing her, would know what had passed between her and Andrew. There was nothing to be done about that; with a shrug she accepted it and left the room.

She was walking down the corridor to the library, where she had last seen Theseus, when Cassia emerged from the quarters she and Tristan had been given. There was no sign of her husband, but the linguist herself looked rested and remarkably unconcerned considering the events of the past few hours.

"How lovely," she said when she caught sight of Marina. "I predict that Atlantan fashions are going to have a strong impact on our own."

"I only wish they could," Marina said, wondering if it was possible that Cassia had somehow misunderstood their situation. That hardly seemed possible, but...

Cassia gave her a reassuring smile, which further baffled Marina. But before she could comment, the other woman said, "Would you be willing to show me around? As prisons go, this place seems extraordinarily luxurious, but I have a feeling that if I start wandering about on my own, I'll promptly get lost."

It was true that this was one of the larger villas. It had been built by Marina's own great-grandfather as a symbol of his family's wealth and power, intended to undermine the ambitions of would-be rivals. When she explained this to Cassia, the other woman laughed. "Human nature really is the same everywhere, isn't it? There are any number of palaces in what you so aptly call the Outer World that were built for the same purpose."

"It is a little odd that Orestes chose to put us here," Marina admitted as they began their tour. Their first stop was the library, which she was surprised to find vacant. "Theseus was here a short time ago. I thought he still would be."

"I think Tristan and Andrew are having a little chat with him."

That was news to Marina. "A chat? What about?"

"Oh...this and that. As for your uncle, I think it's safe to say that he's hedging his bets."

"What do you mean?"

Cassia's attention had been diverted by the floor-to-ceiling shelves of neatly rolled scrolls. Her eyes gleamed, and it was clear that she was itching to delve into them. "What? Oh, your uncle. He's not taking any chances, in case things don't work out the way he's planned. He may be a tough-minded old tyrant," she added with a smile, "but he sure isn't dumb."

"You know," Marina said slowly, looking directly at the other woman, "I'm beginning to realize that there's an awful lot going on that doesn't add up."

Cassia's smile deepened. "Depends on who's doing the adding. Veda, for instance. She can usually make things come out the way she wants them to."

"Veda? How does she come into this?"

"You don't really think she'll let Perseus and the others take *Questor*'s crew by surprise, do you? They'll know they're coming and be fully prepared for them before they get anywhere near the ship."

"But...that's right!" Marina exclaimed. "I had completely forgotten about her, I guess because we don't have anything remotely similar here."

Cassia nodded understandingly. "Which means that Perseus won't have any idea what she is, either. He'll be expecting to have the element of surprise, only to discover that it's been turned against him."

"I only hope," Marina murmured, "that no one gets hurt."

"There is that risk, of course. But I think there's a good chance it will all be settled peacefully."

"Settled how? If your crew does succeed in taking

Perseus and his men prisoner, what will they do with them?''

"I imagine they'll hold them on board while they come after us.''

"You mean they'll attempt a rescue?'' When Cassia nodded, Marina shook her head vehemently. "That's crazy. There's no chance they'll succeed. It's one thing to overcome a small band of warriors, but to go against the entire defense force of Atlantis....'' Visions of what that might mean darted before her eyes. She stiffened and again shook her head. "There must be some way to stop them.''

"There isn't,'' Cassia said calmly. "If my guess is right, they should be here very soon.''

In her agitation, Marina had walked over to one of the library windows. Through it, she spied Tristan, Andrew and Longfellow in close conversation with her brother. As she watched, Theseus nodded several times, made some comment, then smiled broadly. The other three men joined him; then they all shook hands, and Theseus strode off accompanied by Longfellow.

"Excuse me,'' Marina said, turning away from the window and heading for the door.

"Where are you going?'' Cassia asked.

"To the garden, to have a word with Andrew and Tristan. You're welcome to come with me if you like, but I'm going to find out once and for all what's going on here.''

"What's going on,'' Andrew said a few moments later when she confronted him, "is that we've been arranging for a little diversion to give Sean Garrison and the others some help.''

She stared at him for a long moment before the full impact of what he had said sank in. "Theseus. You're going to use him and some of the others who feel as he does to divert Orestes and the defense forces."

At Andrew's curt nod, she went on. "But I told you, there have been several attempted rebellions in the past, and they've all failed."

"Your brother knows that," Andrew said quietly. "He accepts the risk, because he realizes that this time there's a genuine chance of success."

"He accepts it because he wants, more than anything else, to believe that Atlantis can change. But he's going to find out differently. He's going to discover that—"

"That when a new and unexpected element is added to the equation, *everything* changes," Andrew broke in. Against her will, he took her into his arms and, ignoring Tristan and Cassia, said, "I know you're worried about him, and you're angry at me for getting him into this. But it will work out, Marina. Trust me."

She stared back at him doubtfully. Held so close to the warmth and strength of his body, it was difficult for her to think of anything other than her feelings for him. But as much as she loved Andrew, she also loved her brother. And she could not help but believe that Theseus might well be going to his death.

"I have to go after him," she said. "He'll need help, and I can give it."

To her surprise, Andrew didn't argue. Instead he said, "We all can, but first we have to get out of the villa. Cassia, will you stay with Billy and keep in sight of the guards so that they'll think everything is all right?"

"Of course. Much as I'd love to go along, I realize it isn't a good idea in my condition." Tristan put an arm around her and kissed her lightly. His eyes were full of pride as he looked down at her. "You've got a lot of spirit, lady."

"Don't let my brave act fool you," she told him. "You come back in one piece or I'll personally finish you off."

He laughed and patted her gently swollen belly. "It's a deal. You take care of Billy and Junior here, not to mention yourself."

"We have to hurry," Andrew said, loath to interrupt them, but having no choice. "Theseus and his people will be in place shortly."

"I knew he had friends who felt as he did, but I didn't realize they were actually prepared to act," Marina said as the three of them went around the side of the villa to the back entrance Theseus had told them about. Beneath it was a staircase leading to a basement, and in the back of the basement was a tunnel built into the original structure as an escape route for use in times of trouble.

"They've been planning it for some time," Andrew told her. "They've just been waiting for an opportune moment. This is a better chance than they ever could have hoped for."

"Because *Questor*'s crew will be providing a diversion for them," Marina said, "at the same time as they're doing the same in return."

"That's it," Tristan confirmed. "Think of it as a pincer motion, with Orestes caught in the middle."

"I'd love to," Marina said, "but somehow I don't think it will be that simple."

"It won't be," Andrew agreed. "Plenty could go wrong. The point is, it won't—if we do our part."

"Which is?" Marina asked. They had found the entrance to the tunnel without difficulty. She was still marveling at its existence, and wondering how Theseus had known of it, while they were hurrying away from the villa.

"To alert the populace to the existence of the Outer World and the fact that contact has been made. You speculated that most people would approve of that. Let's hope you're right."

"From what Theseus told us," Tristan said, "there's no equivalent to television or radio in Atlantis, so that's out as far as spreading the word goes. But he said something about a sporting event that's being held today and that most of the councillors will be at, including those who weren't told of our arrival."

"The Games," Marina said excitedly. For the first time it occurred to her that their plan might have a chance of succeeding. If they could reach those on the council who opposed Orestes and make the situation clear to them....

"Orestes's strongest opponent on the council," she explained, "is Antigones. Over the years, he's tried repeatedly to unseat my uncle. He'll see this as his best chance ever."

"Then Antigones it is," Andrew said decisively. "Let's find him."

They took one of the monorails into the center of the city, where the stadium was located. Andrew and Tristan's clothing, as well as their dark tans, attracted curious stares, but no one attempted to stop them. They reached the stadium without incident and paused for a moment to listen to the cheers of the crowd from inside.

"Sounds like the home team's winning," Andrew murmured.

"It's the bull dancers," Marina explained. "No one else gets cheers like that."

"Shades of ancient Crete," Tristan said as they passed through the entrance gate. It didn't escape his notice that no tickets were needed.

When he commented on that, Marina said, "The Games are always free. Except for the private boxes, of course, and only the wealthiest people can afford them anyway."

"This Antigones, where will he be?"

"Up there," Marina said, gesturing toward the tier above them, which was lined with private enclosures commanding the best view of the field. "There will be guards," she warned.

"Can you get us past them?" Tristan asked.

After a moment she nodded. "I think so."

They had reached the upper tier and were halfway down the line of boxes when a guard approached them. Marina gave him a dazzling smile and said something that made him laugh, and he stood aside to let them pass.

"What did you tell him?" Andrew murmured when they were safely out of earshot.

"That you were a couple of visitors from the Outer World who wanted to see Antigones."

"He thought that was funny?"

"He thought I was kidding." Rather grimly, she added, "But he's going to find out differently."

The door to the councillor's private box was unguarded; he had clearly thought no further precautions necessary. Marina didn't bother to knock, but instead gestured to them to remain where they were and slipped inside. She was back scant moments later, followed by a middle-aged, somewhat corpulent gentleman with an irate expression.

"I'm not really amused by this, my dear," Antigones said. "This year's bull dancers are by far the best I've ever seen. To be dragged away in the middle of their performance—"

"These men are Outworlders," she said bluntly. "My uncle tried to keep their presence here a secret, but they have escaped from their guards and arranged for my brother to lead a rebellion as soon as the force coming to rescue them arrives."

"W-what...?" the councillor stuttered, staring at them. Andrew had a quick, amusing revelation of what it would be like for the first alien to arrive on earth and announce his presence. He would undoubtedly be met with similar eloquence.

"Outw-worlders," Antigones said, clearly stunned. He stared from one to the other of them as both Andrew and Tristan endeavored to look suitably impressive. "I've dreamed, of course...longed for the day," Antigones continued, "but I never really imagined..."

"The day has come," Marina told him flatly. "There is no turning back. The question is how to rally the people to accept what has happened. If the rebellion fails, or the Outworlders are harmed, the consequences will be dire."

"That mustn't happen!" Antigones exclaimed. "We all know how dangerous they are. Orestes is a fool to invite their retribution." He cast a quick look at Andrew and Tristan, as though hoping he hadn't offended them.

"There will be no need for any," Andrew said carefully, "provided the proper steps are taken."

"Of course, of course," Antigones said. Already he

was rubbing his hands together with ill-disguised eagerness. "I'll call an assembly. As councillor, I have the right."

"Assembly?" Tristan queried.

Marina explained. "Of all the leading citizens of Atlantis. It's been done in the past when a matter of particular seriousness has to be clarified. Once your presence is revealed there, Orestes will be unable to deny it."

"Then get on with it, man," Andrew said. "We've got no time to lose."

The councillor scurried away even as Marina noticed out of the corner of her eye that the guard was returning. "It looks as though he's decided it might not be a joke after all. Let's get going."

They did as she suggested and were quickly out of the stadium. Andrew understood the need for haste, but under different circumstances he wouldn't have minded lingering. The single glimpse he'd had of a young man hurtling over the horns of a bull had been tantalizing.

"Where to?" Marina asked as soon as they were safely back on the street.

"The dock where we arrived," Andrew said. "That's where the sub will be coming in."

Using the monorail again, it took them about half an hour to reach the edge of the city, and a further few minutes to make their way on foot to the dock. They were approaching it confidently when the low sound of gunfire reverberated in the quiet air. For an instant they froze; then, without exchanging a word, they broke into a run.

Chapter 16

"It's okay," Sean Garrison told them when they burst onto the dock where he and several other members of the *Questor*'s crew were holding a pair of guards at gunpoint. "We only fired to warn them off. Though having gotten a look at that Perseus character, I didn't really count on it working. It did give us a few seconds' edge to disarm them, though."

"Nice plan," Andrew said as he accepted one of the guards' confiscated lasers from Sean and strapped it around his waist. He hoped he wouldn't be called on to use it, but he felt better being armed. "Have any trouble getting here?"

Sean shook his head. "Not once we realized Veda wasn't kidding. Rather than take the chance of anyone getting hurt, I told her to drop the oxygen content in the sub's air far enough to make them woozy. Worked like a charm."

"Let's hope the rest of it does," Tristan said as he

strapped on the other weapon. "Cassia and Billy are at a villa a short distance outside the city."

Sean whistled softly under his breath. "Any ideas how we're going to get there and back without being stopped?"

"We're betting," Andrew told him, "that folks around here are going to be too busy to be very interested in anything we're doing."

At Sean's quizzical look, he said, "I'll explain later." He gestured toward the guards. "Let's get these two comfortable and then move out."

Moments later the guards were securely bound and gagged and stashed in a small supply closet. As the second of them was pushed inside, he muttered something to Marina.

"What did he say?" Andrew asked as they were leaving the low stone building that housed the air lock.

"Nothing important." She was flushing slightly, but hoped he wouldn't notice.

He had; he noticed everything about her. He said grimly, "Tell me."

Reluctantly, she murmured, "He merely called my virtue into question."

"The hell he did!" Instinctively, he half turned back toward the dock.

"Don't," she said, laying a hand on his arm. "It doesn't matter."

"Oh, really? I got the impression that it mattered rather a lot to you."

The color deepened in her high-boned cheeks. His reminder of her recently lost virginity brought with it other memories she was trying desperately to ignore. "What counts is getting Cassia and Billy away from the villa. If Theseus's plan fails, they'll have no other chance of escape.''

He hardly had to be told that, but it was still extremely difficult to do as she asked. His hands itched to reach around the other man's neck even as he realized that the guard who had insulted her was undoubtedly only one of many who would take the same attitude.

Though there was a tremendous amount he did not yet understand about the Atlantans, he already realized that they were a conservative people who lived by a strict moral code. Marina had violated it when she yielded to the passion between them. Silently, he vowed that he would do anything within his power to make sure that she didn't regret what they had shared.

But first there was the small matter of a rebellion to get through.

As they exited onto the street, they heard shouting and the sounds of running feet. Several men ran by, taking no notice of them in their rush. They were followed by perhaps a dozen more, these in the uniform of the Atlantan guard.

''It's begun,'' Marina murmured on a note of wonder. Though she hadn't doubted Theseus's intentions for a moment, she had scarcely believed that he could carry them through. Yet that appeared to be precisely the case.

She shouted a question, and in response a young man paused long enough to yell, ''It's rebellion! Theseus Lirularia has taken the council chamber with his fellows. They hold Orestes and the others. Antigones has called an assembly. Something great is in the wind!''

''Go on to the villa,'' Marina said when she had quickly translated this for Andrew and the others.

"Find Cassia and Billy, and get them back here." As Andrew was about to object, she said, "There's still no guarantee this will work. I must go to the council chamber to add my voice to Theseus's. When I tell them that I've actually been outside, and that the people there are very much like us, there's a chance Orestes will agree to continued contact."

"And if he doesn't?" Andrew demanded. "Or if they simply don't believe you?"

"I have to risk that," she told him, her head high in defiance of her fear. It was possible these were the last moments they would have together. She reached out in instinctive protest, but let her hand fall short of touching him. Instead she turned and hurried away before her heart could overrule her mind.

The council chamber was in chaos when Marina reached it. A cordon of Theseus's friends surrounded it, armed with lasers and wearing the tense air of men who knew their actions to be momentous. She was quickly allowed to pass, though the young man who was apparently in charge said, "Orestes's guards haven't surrendered yet. They may not let you through."

"I'll chance it," she said. Steadily, she approached the building. She could hear raised voices, and she recognized her uncle and Antigones, both talking at the same time and at cross purposes.

The commander of the guards was an older man, not unlike Perseus in appearance and manner. She guessed that he had been summoned at the first sign of the rebellion and had taken up his post with the absolute intention of holding it to the death. But he was also a realist, and when she told him that she had information the council needed to hear, he let her pass, but not without a warning.

"They may not be willing to listen, lady. Tempers are running high."

"I don't doubt it," she said with a faint smile. "What they need is something to cool them."

He was clearly inclined to agree, though far too well-disciplined to give in to any such desire. He did, however, assure her that she would be allowed to enter the building without being stopped again.

Once inside, she paused and glanced around a bit uncertainly. People were milling about in front of the council chamber. She recognized several of Theseus's friends, as well as friends of her uncle. Both sides were evidently well represented, but there was no sign of the major adversaries themselves.

By dint of pressing herself forward against the crowd, she managed at last to reach the doors of the council chamber and slip beyond them. Inside, the atmosphere was, if anything, worse. People stood around in clusters, hollering at each other at the top of their lungs, completely ignoring the fierce debate going on toward the front.

"Admit your defeat!" Theseus was demanding. He stood with his feet planted squarely apart, one hand resting on the laser at his hip, facing his uncle angrily. "You attempted to deceive us for your own purposes, but you failed. We know about the Outworlders, and we demand the chance to decide for ourselves what should be done about them."

"Fools!" Orestes hurled back. "You think you have the wisdom for such a decision? You are nothing but callow youths bent on making names for yourselves. You aren't thinking about what's good for Atlantis."

"What's good," Theseus countered, "is to stop hiding and admit that we're part of a larger world that, for better or worse, has people in it who aren't very different from ourselves. We were part of it once. We must be again!"

Orestes had been sitting in solemn dignity in the highest chair on the dais, but now he rose, shaking with fury, and confronted the younger men. "Was it for this that our ancestors defied death, vanquished their own terrors, even triumphed over nature itself? So that their descendants could betray everything they achieved?"

"You are the betrayer," Theseus shot back. "You have forgotten the immense courage it took to survive, to build our world. It was founded on faith in our ability to overcome any challenge, no matter how great. We did so four thousand years ago, and we will do so today." Turning to the gathering of those who had been caught by the exchange and stood now in rapt attention, he said, "I call for the resignation of the high councillor. He no longer represents the will of the Atlantans, and he must therefore be replaced."

Quickly, as though out of the very air itself, the chant was taken up. "Resign! Resign!"

Orestes paled. He saw the mood of the crowd turning against him and was at a loss as to how to stop it. Then he caught sight of Marina. "Wait!" he shouted. "Here is one who can tell you the truth. She has been to the Outer World itself. She has seen it for what it really is. Marina, speak!"

Caught off guard, she stood wide-eyed in the center of a raptly attentive audience. All around her she heard the eager murmurs of those who waited for her to relate what she had learned.

With no time to prepare, Marina was at a loss as to

how to begin. She struggled to gather her thoughts and speak in terms that would be meaningful to both sides in the confrontation.

"It is true," she began softly, "that the Outer World is very different from our own. Yet there is also much that we share." She could feel the quiet spreading through the chamber as those who were still talking among themselves were hushed by others. Gaining confidence, she spoke more firmly. "I am a woman, not a warrior, and therefore what I have to relate may not be what you consider to be important. But I ask that you open your hearts as well as your minds to the truth I tell."

The faces of the men, suffused with anger as they hovered on the edge of violence only a few moments before, now showed tolerance, if not softening. She had wooed them with her deference and made them willing to listen.

"I met a child in the Outer World," she continued slowly. "His name is Billy. He's three years old, and for most of that time his mother has been dead. Because of the way things are there, his father has raised him. He worries about whether or not he is doing right by his son. He wants him to grow into a good, strong man, which is what he is himself. I think his hopes for Billy are the same as any of you would have for your own sons."

In the faces watching her—young and old, smooth-skinned and weathered—she saw agreement. These were men who cared about children, both their own and others'. They could understand the worry of a father, and the dreams.

"Andrew—that's Billy's father—wants his son to grow up in a world at peace. He and many others are working very hard to bring that about. They acknowledge the mistakes that have been made in the past, and they want to prevent them from being repeated in the future.''

''Then why do they build weapons that can destroy the world itself?'' Orestes demanded. He had stepped down from the dais and now strode into the center of the chamber near where Marina stood. The assembly instinctively cleared a space for them. Theseus remained off to one side, watching his sister intently.

''I think they have done so out of fear,'' she answered quietly. ''Fear of themselves, and of each other.'' For a moment she hesitated, wondering how far she could go with these proud men. But truth had become its own compulsion, and she could not back away from it now. ''We know what that is like, for it is fear that has kept us hidden here all these centuries.''

A low grumble of dissent threatened to grow into much more, but Marina cut it off swiftly. ''I mean no insult. There is no one who would question the courage of any man here.'' That much was also true. ''But fear,'' she went on, ''can come on us unknowingly. It can become a habit that we find very hard to break.''

Orestes looked as though he was about to challenge her again, but then appeared to think better of it. She could read confusion in his eyes, and in the eyes of many of his supporters. It came to her that they had expected her to present a view of the Outer World so one-sided as to be easily exposed for the fantasy it would have been. But instead she had admitted to the problems that existed, calling on them to work for solutions rather than merely allow things to go on as they had for too long.

''Marina is right,'' Theseus said, stepping into the

circle. "Fear is no more than a habit. We can make the decision to change right now by voting to establish contact with the Outer World."

The men glanced at one another anxiously. Most had entered the chamber with a firm idea of where they stood on so momentous an issue, but faced with actually voting their convictions, they were no longer as certain. Particularly not in light of the appeal Marina had made.

"We don't want to be too hasty about this," Antigones ventured in a seeming reversal that was nonetheless in keeping with his cautious character. Marina almost smiled as she recognized the conflict within him. It was one thing for a man to nurture a dream that made him feel daring, even romantic. It was quite another to confront that dream made real.

"Once contact is established," Antigones went on, "it can never again be withdrawn. How do we know that the Outworlders, who greatly surpass us in number, may not attempt to conquer us?"

"Let them try," Theseus said with the quick, confident laugh of a young man who yearns to face some great test. "Their weapons make them no more than helpless giants, since they cannot use them against each other or against us without destroying themselves as well. *That* is their fear. Like us, they want to live, to see their children grow, to glimpse a better future."

"Perhaps," Orestes said thoughtfully, "we can help them achieve that. After all, we have lived in peace for thousands of years. Who knows it better than us?"

Marina forgave him the slight note of pomposity in his voice. She alone among the gathering knew that once the men of Atlantis made contact with the Outer World, they were in for some surprises that would, to say the least, shake them out of their complacency. The peace Orestes spoke of so confidently might be lacking in more than a few households once word spread of certain other differences Marina had not chosen to mention.

While all this was under rapt discussion, a messenger approached from the side of the council chamber and handed a slip of paper to Orestes. He read it, frowning.

"It appears," he said, "that our confidence in our ability to deal with the Outworlders may be misplaced. Commander Perseus and his crew have apparently been captured."

In the wake of the shocked exclamations that greeted this revelation, he continued. "A party of Outworlders is loose in the city. They disarmed and confined two guards who attempted to stop them. Further, the Outworlder captives are missing from the villa where they were being held, and the pod they arrived in is also missing."

Orestes turned a stern eye on Theseus. "What have you to do with this? I presumed you and your sister escaped with the aid of your confederates, but now it appears that more is involved."

"You could hardly expect the Outworlders to meekly accept imprisonment," Theseus asserted. "They are men like us; naturally, they sought to free themselves."

Around the chamber, heads nodded. This, too, they could understand. As could Marina. Yet though she tried to be glad their plan had worked, she couldn't stem the tide of sorrow threatening to engulf her.

Andrew was gone, back to the world they had so briefly shared. Even if the assembly did vote to establish contact, there was no guarantee that they could pick up their relationship where it had ended. On the contrary, she had good reason to believe that would never be possible.

It would be many years, if ever, before the peoples of the Inner and Outer worlds would be able to reconcile their differences and come together as one. Until then, they would in many respects be aliens to each other. She could easily forget that, so great was the power of her love, but she didn't expect Andrew to be able to do the same. If nothing else, he certainly would not soon forget that her mere presence in his world had endangered both himself and his son.

She couldn't blame him in any way, but she could wish that there had been some last word for her, anything that would have let her believe that their joining had not been completely unimportant to him.

Instead there was only silence and a looming sense of emptiness against which the excited voices once again filling the council chamber were no more than the hollow murmurs of a fathomless sea cave.

Chapter 17

"This is a hell of a situation," David Longfellow said pleasantly as he sat sprawled on the couch in Andrew's living room. Hildy had returned and was in the kitchen making chocolate chip cookies for Billy, who continued to regale her with details of his visit to Atlantis. Andrew knew his housekeeper had no more idea what to make of the story than most people did. Despite the stories in the newspaper, and on television and radio, word of Atlantis's existence had provoked surprisingly little excitement.

Although perhaps it wasn't so surprising, Andrew thought as he kept one ear on what the security man was saying but let his mind wander free. People could see and hear far more remarkable things than that simply by going to a movie or picking up a book. It was an age seemingly immune to awe and conditioned to look outward rather than inward.

Only a relatively small number of people—mainly

scientists of various sorts—had grasped the importance of the discovery and were champing at the bit to get a look at Atlantis for themselves. But to ordinary people enmeshed in the problems of their own lives, it was strictly a one-day wonder.

"What did you think of the Senate debate?" Longfellow was asking. "If some of those guys had their way, this whole thing would be brushed under the carpet."

"That could still happen," Andrew pointed out. "The president has yet to name even the first of the emissaries Orestes asked for."

"It works both ways. The exalted high councillor hasn't named his people yet, either."

Andrew shook his head wearily. He had been sleeping very badly and didn't have to seek far to find the explanation. His dreams were an enticing torment of memory and desire. Waking from them, he invariably found himself both cursing Marina and longing for her.

He had to stop that. She was back where she belonged, and so was he. They had come from separate worlds, and they had returned to them. The sooner he accepted that and got over her, the better.

Except that he might as well have contemplated getting over the need to breathe. Smothering a sigh, he glanced out toward the patio. The previous evening he and Billy had stood out there along with the bird the little boy had found. It had, thanks to Marina's care, fully recovered. When Billy had lifted it in his hands and slowly opened them, the dove hadn't moved for a moment. Instead it had looked from the boy to the man and back again, as though in silent acknowledgment that their lives and its had, however briefly, intertwined.

With a bob of its head, it had lifted its wings and caught the wind. Only the slightest bit, of course, because it wasn't a grand bird, like an eagle or a hawk, but only a small brown creature that lived close to the earth and made a pleasant cooing sound as it went about its business.

Andrew thought he could hear it now, though it might have been any one of its numerous cousins. For a few months more they would linger on Angle Key. Then these non-eagles would take to the sky, flying thousands of miles to their summer fields. More than a few would die in the process, but none would turn back.

"You've got to give Orestes credit, though," Longfellow said. "I didn't figure he'd be able to hold on after that rebellion Theseus led."

"Actually, it makes perfect sense that he'd remain in office," Andrew replied. "Now that the Atlantans are face-to-face with an enormous change, they're less inclined to make any others. Orestes is their assurance of at least some continuity."

Longfellow nodded thoughtfully. He had made the trip down from Washington only that day and was tired. Andrew had offered him the guest room, which he'd accepted gratefully. But before he could retire for some much-needed rest, he had a mission to complete.

"Tristan's going to be named to the delegation," he told Andrew. "That's definite, even though it isn't official yet. They're also trying to convince Cassia to come on board, but she's reluctant."

"Why?" Andrew asked. His parting from the Wards had been hasty; they had been hustled off to Washington, and he returned home to the news that his equations had, as he had suspected, led to a breakthrough in the defense system. It was in its final stages now, but Andrew was no longer involved. His work done, he was content to step back and let others claim the glory that would come when the system was at last operative.

"She doesn't want to take on anything that could get in the way of her pregnancy," Longfellow explained. "I guess the kid is pretty important to her."

"They all are," Andrew said quietly. In his mind's eye, he was seeing the sketches of how the defense network would look when it was installed. Against the blackness of space, small silver eyes would glitter, not unlike the many-eyed Argus the ancient Greeks had worshiped. Like that all-seeing creature they would, thanks to the breakthroughs that had been made, keep watch over a world in which the potential for self-destruction was rapidly being neutralized.

"I suppose you know," Longfellow said, "that the Russians are just about ready, too."

"I heard something to that effect," Andrew acknowledged. In actual fact, there would be two systems, one for each of the superpowers that had glowered at each other with so much suspicion for so long. By virtue of the shared supply of xanium and an equal degree of creativity on the part of their scientists, the systems were remarkably similar. Already there was talk that the day would come when they were combined for the shared protection of a world at peace.

"It's not going to be the same," Longfellow mused, not without a certain note of regret. "Maybe it's just as well this Atlantis thing came along. It'll be a long time before we get anything settled there."

"Sounds as though you're hoping there will be problems."

Longfellow shot him a crooked grin. "Hey, I don't want to find myself out of a job. Besides, there's a ton of stuff to be worked out. Just figuring out trade arrangements will keep us busy for quite a while. Then there's the exchange of scientific information, access to historical archives, the whole telepathy thing. Not to mention that energy source of theirs that Orestes didn't care to reveal."

"They sure do use a lot of energy," Andrew agreed pleasantly.

"Think it's fusion?"

"Could be."

"If they've licked that..."

"Of course, it could be something we've never even thought of. Maybe something that's not dangerous, doesn't pollute and goes on forever."

"You really think there's a chance of that?"

Andrew shrugged. "Should be worth looking into."

"Yeah...but we'd need a guy who would know what he was seeing."

"There are plenty of qualified scientists who would jump at the chance."

"The problem is," Longfellow explained glumly, "the Atlantans aren't too eager to approve delegates they don't know."

Andrew turned and looked at him. After a moment, he said, "Why am I getting the idea that you didn't just drop in for a friendly chat?"

"I know I gave you that impression when I arrived, but..."

"Don't you ever play straight on anything?"

"Well...no, actually. It would be sort of out of character, wouldn't it."

Andrew muttered something rude and stood up. His

hands were thrust deeply into the pockets of his jeans, stretching them taut over his lean hips and powerful thighs. "I don't want to discuss it."

Another man would have taken the hint, but not Longfellow. Imperturbably, he said, "Why not? It's a natural for you."

"No, it isn't."

"Wait a sec…let me guess. It's the girl, isn't it? Marina." Longfellow whistled softly. "She's some knockout."

"Are you finished?"

"You're kidding? I'm barely getting wound up. So that's the problem. Well, hell, it ought to be easy enough to fix. Take the job, go on back there, give her the whole nine yards and see what develops."

"It's good to know," Andrew said grimly, "that a man with your, shall we say, simple approach can still get ahead in the world."

"I do all right, which, if you don't mind my saying so, is more than you can claim at the moment."

"And what," Andrew demanded, "is that supposed to mean?"

"Only that I've seen happier faces on corpses. You're eating yourself up alive over her, when all you have to do is go for it."

"I told you I didn't want to discuss this."

"Hey," Longfellow said, holding up his hands in a placating gesture, "if you're that scared…"

"I'm not."

"Oh, yeah? Boy, I sure would be. Any woman that terrific would scare me to death. Fortunately—or unfortunately, depending on how you look at it—I don't have that problem. But you do. So what do you say to doing something about it and helping us out in the bargain?''

What he thought, Andrew decided much later that day, when everyone else was asleep and he was nursing a short brandy in the den, was that he had to be out of his mind. He had barely managed to survive Elizabeth's death and put his life back into some semblance of order. That had been tough enough. Getting over Marina would be just about beyond him.

So why was the thought of seeing her again irresistible?

The answer wasn't long in coming to him. When it did, he smiled in wry amusement at himself and the vagaries of fate. Love was one part of life's equation he would never fully understand. Still, it was time to stop pretending it didn't lie at the center of what Longfellow would undoubtedly call ''the whole ball of wax.''

''How would you feel about my going away for a few days?'' he asked Billy the next morning at the breakfast table. Longfellow had taken himself off, undoubtedly to get into some kind of mischief Andrew would rather not know about. Hildy was bustling around at the stove, but he suspected she had one ear usefully cocked.

''Go with you?'' Billy asked hopefully.

Andrew hesitated. He adored his son, but he felt he needed time alone with Marina if they were to work out their problems. ''I think,'' he said gently, ''that it would be better for you to stay here. I won't be gone long, and maybe when I come back I'll have some good news.'' He hadn't wanted to say even that much, always believing that it was wrong to raise false hopes in a child, but the look in Billy's eyes made him take the chance.

His son smiled and nodded his small head vigorously. "You're going back to 'lantis?"

"That's right. Just for a short visit this time, but I may be going there regularly. If that happens, you'll come with me."

"See Marina. Good."

"I hope so," Andrew murmured, not wanting to raise false hopes in himself, either.

"Is that the young lady who was staying here?" Hildy asked as she set a plate of bacon and eggs in front of him. She was an amply built lady of uncertain years and very certain opinions. Andrew had long since gotten used to her speaking her mind.

"Yes," he said as he sprinkled pepper on his eggs. "She's from there."

"Billy speaks well of her."

"She's…a very special person."

Hildy sniffed and turned back to the stove, but not before he saw the smile creasing her broad face. "I'll be going to the market today. Best add pepper to the shopping list."

He glanced down at his eggs, saw that he had made them inedible, and sighed. Pushing the plate away, he said, "I wasn't really hungry anyway."

Hildy nodded sagely. "Takes some people like that."

"What does?" As though he didn't know.

"Pretty young things with big green eyes and long black hair who walk around with no clothes on." She giggled vigorously enough to shake her round frame. "Maybe I should go see my sister again. Things seem to get real interesting around here when I'm gone."

"That won't be necessary," Andrew said with great dignity. He rose, patted his avidly listening son on the head, and went to pack.

Whatever else could be said about Orestes, when he made up his mind to something, he didn't hold back. The delegation headed by the United States Secretary of State and comprised in equal numbers of diplomats and scientists was received with all possible pomp. Courtesies were exchanged at dockside, followed by a cavalcade along streets lined by a cheering crowd.

The Atlantans seemed genuinely glad to see them, though Andrew suspected that such welcomes would quickly lose their novelty. Delegations were due shortly from Great Britain, France and the Soviet Union. The Chinese had ventured that it was possible they had once had trade agreements with Atlantis and were preparing to renegotiate them. The greatest excitement, of course, could be found in Greece, where plans were well underway for what was aptly being called a re-union.

But perhaps the most surprising news came from a group of Mexican anthropologists who had found evidence of an Aztec-Atlantan connection that appeared to *postdate* the submergence. That raised the possibility that survivors had reached Central America, and opened up an entirely new line of inquiry for both peoples to pursue.

The welcome concluded with a state dinner in the council hall. Andrew sat through a series of typically stultifying speeches with growing impatience. He had yet to catch even a glimpse of Marina. Her brother was on hand, but seemed to be deliberately keeping his distance. Orestes, too, had shot Andrew a look that suggested the older man was thinking of giving him a piece of his mind.

Or perhaps he was merely imagining both men's reactions. His feelings for Marina were occupying virtually all his attention, but the rest of the world had its own concerns. Life went on, however bumpily.

The Secretary of State had at last concluded his remarks and sat down. The first of what promised to be many courses appeared, and the company fell to with a will. Plentiful translators had been provided, but a surprising number of the Atlantans were, if not fluent in English, close to it. Andrew gathered from remarks he overheard that such widespread ability had come as a surprise to their government, which had belatedly realized that its attempts to control information had not been as successful as had been believed.

Tristan was deep in an involved discussion about hydroponic agriculture with several Atlantan scientists. Andrew was dutifully trying to listen when he happened to glance up as Marina entered the chamber. She stood in the doorway, a vision in an off-the-shoulder tunic of royal blue shot through with gold. She had left her hair down, but had secured it back from her brow with a fillet of gold and emeralds. Her skin shone like polished alabaster, and when she moved the tunic flowed against her to reveal the slender, graceful lines of her body.

Without realizing that he was doing so, Andrew stood up. Tristan shot him a startled glance, turned in the direction he was looking, and grinned. He went back to his conversation with the scientists as Andrew moved purposefully away from the table.

Marina saw him coming toward her at the precise

moment that she was considering changing her mind about attending the dinner and leaving instead. Her uncle had insisted that she should be there, and she was loath to disappoint him when they were suddenly getting along so well. But the strain of enduring hours in the same room with Andrew, however large it was and however many other people were present, seemed beyond her.

She had learned of his presence in the delegation not with surprise but with a certain feeling of resignation tinged by hope she could not deny, no matter how inappropriate it was. She had thought she had steeled herself against the necessity of seeing him again, but that wasn't proving to be the case. Yet she could hardly retreat ignominiously.

She was still hesitating, uncertain of what to do, when she spied Andrew striding toward her from across the room. For a moment her breath caught in her throat. He was normally dressed in a dark gray suit, with his thick amber hair combed back from his powerful features and his dark eyes alight with a look she had never seen before, and she was powerless to draw away from him.

He reached her side and held out a hand. Without thinking, she put hers in it. "You're beautiful," he said softly, his eyes drinking her in.

Her own were fastened on the firm line of his mouth. She watched his lips move, thought of them moving over her, and flushed. "T-thank you. I—" With an effort, she wrenched her gaze away and looked around the room a bit frantically. "Is Theseus here?"

Andrew did not move, nor did he release her hand. He merely tilted his head in the direction of the dais. "Over there somewhere. He's trying to explain to one of the members of our delegation why there aren't more women present at this dinner.''

Despite herself, Marina smiled. "I wonder what he thinks of the explanation."

"She," Andrew corrected with a grin. "She's an assistant Secretary of State who's lobbied hard for women's rights around the world. She's also not hard to look at."

Marina raised her eyebrows and peered more intently toward the dais. Just as he'd said, she could see her brother in rapt conversation with a slender young woman of about thirty-five with dark red hair, lovely features, and, if only from the waist up, a very nice figure. It appeared that they were arguing.

She laughed softly. "Poor Theseus. He may just have met his match."

"Why should I be the only one?" Andrew murmured. At her startled glance, he said, "Let's get out of here."

"You mean not attend the dinner?"

"You don't really think we'll be missed, do you?"

"No," she admitted. "I guess not." The thought of being alone with him made her heart beat painfully. She wanted to refuse, to walk away from him as quickly as she could, but she couldn't bring herself to take even the first step.

"Are you still staying at the villa?" he asked as his hand slipped up to cup her elbow and turn her gently toward the door.

She nodded. "We've been having so many meetings that it's more convenient to be close by."

"I take it we won't be disturbed there?"

She nodded again, no longer making any attempt to deny, even to herself, that this was what she wanted.

Undoubtedly this would make it even more difficult to get over him, but she would deal with that when she had to.

The villa was virtually deserted. Even the guards were absent, since they were no longer considered necessary. They walked down a long gravel path bordered by oleander trees and entered through a side door. Their footsteps echoed on the mosaic floor.

The silence between them was maintained until they reached Marina's room. When the door had closed behind them, Andrew laid his hands gently on her shoulders and looked deeply into her eyes.

"We really have to talk," he murmured.

Her moist lips parted slightly. She raised herself on her toes and touched her mouth to his. Her breath was a whisper on the scented air. "Later."

Chapter 18

Out of darkness came light. At first it came tentatively, reminding Marina of the sky when only a handful of stars shone. From that small beginning were galaxies born. She fell headlong into the heart of creation and found within it the other half of herself.

She had heard so much about the joining, already experienced so much. Yet so much had remained to be discovered.

She had taken a chance, but only afterward did she realize how great the risk had been. Once joined in this way, she and Andrew would never again be fully separate, no matter how much time and distance might lie between them.

She trembled slightly as he passed a gentle hand down between the cleft of her breasts to the flat plane of her belly. Her skin glistened, as did his. The harsh sound of their breathing still filled the shadowed chamber.

He had raised himself up on one arm, and now he touched his mouth tenderly to hers. "I think," he said softly, "that I understand why all this has happened."

"You mean to us?" she asked.

He shook his head. "To Atlantis. Why it was submerged, why a small number of people survived, why they remained here all these generations."

Her lips, still brushing his, formed a single word. "Why?"

"So that this—what do you call it—joining could come into being."

Joining. She had never mentioned the word to him, and she was certain no one else would have brought up such a private subject. Which left only one explanation for how he could have learned it.

"What else," she asked quietly, "did you find in my mind?"

He lay back against the pillows and stared up at the ceiling. "The same thing you must have found in mine: love."

Only then did she dare to admit to herself what she had touched. The poignant beauty of it brought tears to her eyes. For once, she didn't try to hold them back.

There was no sound to alert him, but still he knew. He turned again, and his fingers brushed against her cheeks. She felt the question he didn't have to ask.

"It's all right," she murmured. "They aren't sad tears."

He sighed deeply, and her heart tightened. She didn't want him to feel any sense of obligation to her. That was the surest way to kill love. But when he spoke, she had to quickly revise her opinion of what concerned him.

"You know," he said, "there have been men and

women who have managed to overcome the differences between them and build a life together.'' Before she could comment, he went on hurriedly. ''I realize none of them faced a situation quite like ours, but I still think we could come to some...arrangement.''

''What do you mean?'' she asked, surprised by her own daring.

Instead of answering directly, he said, ''Do you know the legend of Persephone? It's part of Greek mythology, so you might be familiar with it.''

''Of course. She was a goddess of fertility, supposedly abducted by Pluto, who kept her with him in the underworld for four months of each year.'' A soft laugh broke from her, born of the beginnings of hope. ''Are you comparing me to the king of Hades?''

''I was thinking more of myself,'' he assured her. ''It occurred to me that I might be able to persuade you to continue your study of the Outer World.''

''Why...would you want to?''

''Because if I can give you a reason for spending part of each year there, I thought I might be able to convince you to marry me.''

''M-marry?''

''You do have marriage here, don't you?'' It hadn't occurred to him that he might have to explain what that meant. Fortunately, it seemed that wouldn't be necessary after all.

''Of course we do, but...it's different here.''

''How so?''

''It's more...serious. I heard on the television about something you call divorce.''

His brow furrowed. She'd learned more than he had thought, including a few things he wished could have waited. ''What about it?''

"We don't have it, though perhaps we should consider it, since it's true that some marriages simply don't
work out. But if we did, it would still be very rare here.
In your world, it seems to be very common."

"I suppose it is," he admitted. "But what's that got
to do with us?"

"Nothing, I hope. My point is, though, that I could
never...that is..." The last thing she wanted to do was
to make him feel trapped, yet she had to be honest with
him if they were to have any chance. "I would rather
never see you again," she finally managed to say,
"than run the risk that what we feel for each other
might not be enough to bridge the differences between
us."

He was silent for a long moment. When he finally
spoke, she could hear the anger in his voice. "I didn't
realize you were a coward."

"I'm not," she protested vehemently. "How can
you say such a thing?"

"Because you're as afraid to take a risk as all the
rest of your people. You'd rather stay in your safe little
world where nothing can hurt you." He rolled over
abruptly, pinning her under him. His weight was heavy
on her, but she barely noticed it. All her attention was
focused on the waves of hurt she felt emanating from
him.

"I've got news for you, lady," he muttered. "That
safe little world has been shattered, and there's no putting it back together again. You've got to deal with
things the way they are, whether you want to or not,
and the fact is that I'm not about to let you walk
away."

"I didn't say I wanted to...."

"You didn't say 'yes,' either. I ask you to marry me,

and you start talking about divorce. That's just a bit premature, wouldn't you say?''

His sarcasm wounded her deeply even as she realized the source of it. The joining, it seemed, was not the perfect conduit to mutual understanding that she had imagined. There were still things that had to be brought out into the open and talked about.

''All right,'' she said. ''I am afraid. We come from different worlds, and there are bound to be misunderstandings between us. All I meant was that when I marry, it has to be forever.''

He glared down at her, a muscle beating in his jaw. ''Fine with me.''

''It is?'' She couldn't quite conceal her shock. He gave every indication of meaning exactly what he said.

''How long does it take to arrange a wedding around here?''

''Oh, lord,'' she murmured, closing her eyes, ''I didn't think of that.''

''Of what?''

''Marriage involving a wedding.''

''You know of some other way to do it?''

''You don't understand. Weddings are...very complicated here. For one thing—'' she hesitated, imagining how he would react ''—you're going to have to go talk with Uncle Orestes. Not only that,'' she added hurriedly, ''but I suspect Theseus will want to be involved, too.''

His slashing grin warned her of what was coming. ''Are you telling me that I have to ask your uncle's permission to marry you, and possibly also your brother's?''

''It's the custom,'' she murmured defensively.

''Are they...uh...likely to refuse?''

Her smile matched his own, carrying with it a wealth of love and joy. "I rather think they'll be glad to get me off their hands."

His unabashedly masculine laughter irked her. She was about to reprove him for it when she seemed to lose her train of thought. It was very difficult to keep a clear head, much less be angry, when his hands and mouth had begun once again to wreak delightful havoc on her body. How much simpler to succumb and, in the process, to triumph.

"Well, my boy," Orestes said with ponderous care, "you've made your intentions clear. Now let us discuss your prospects."

Andrew stifled the impulse to ask if he would also like to check his teeth and instead summoned all his patience. The interview he had thought would be so amusing was turning out to be anything but. Orestes, it seemed, was deadly serious about withholding his approval of their marriage until he was certain it was justified.

"I realize," the high councillor went on, "that your ways are different from our own, but, as Marina's eldest male relative, I am naturally concerned about her well-being."

"I understand, sir, but I assure you, you have nothing to worry about."

"She is rather…high-spirited. Will you be able to control that?"

"Frankly, I wouldn't want to. I love Marina just the way she is. As far as her high spirits go, they always seem to be leavened by good judgment."

"Hmm," Orestes murmured noncommittally. With more tact than might have been expected, he changed the subject. "You have a young son, I believe. Will he accept Marina as his mother?"

"I think he already has," Andrew said, remembering Billy's wholehearted joy when he had joined his father and learned that he and Marina were going to be married. "Billy took to Marina immediately," he explained. "He loves her very much, as she does him."

"And what about other children?" Orestes inquired. "Do you wish to have them?"

"Yes, but not right away. Marina and I have talked about this, and we decided it would be best to wait a couple of years until we've had a chance to settle in together."

"Don't wait too long," Orestes advised. "It's best to keep a woman like Marina well occupied with children."

Andrew could no longer hide a grin. "If you don't mind my saying so, sir, you're what we call a male chauvinist back home."

"I heard that phrase recently," Orestes said with a frown. "Now where was that...?"

"Possibly from a young woman who's a member of our delegation?"

"Oh, yes. She was hollering it at Theseus, as a matter of fact. Do I take it she wasn't being complimentary?"

"Let's just say that her diplomatic skills must be fraying around the edges."

"Theseus has been known to have that effect on people. Now about your prospects...."

"I manage to stay gainfully employed, and I make a good living. My investments are sound. I suppose I'm what people would call affluent."

"That never hurts. Marina is accustomed to certain comforts."

"So I've noticed, sir. Is there…uh…anything else?"

Orestes thought for a moment, then shook his head. "No, I think that covers everything. You have my permission to wed Marina."

After Andrew had thanked him with proper gravity, Orestes summoned a servant, who brought drinks for them both. The two men drank a toast to the soon-to-be bride, after which Orestes smiled benignly.

"I understand," he said to Andrew, "that you've accepted a permanent position on your delegation. Does that mean you will be here fairly frequently?"

"About half of each year, sir. Marina and I plan to spend the other half mainly on Angle Key, where I have a house."

"I see…and while you are here, what in particular will you be interested in?"

Andrew hesitated. He felt he had to choose his words with care so as not to warn Orestes off. "It's my hope to facilitate scientific exchange. We have technologies you may find useful, and I'm sure the reverse is also true."

"Hmm, yes, I rather suspect it is." Orestes put down his drink and reached for a small black box that had been resting on the inlaid marble table at his side. "Allow me to present you with an early wedding gift," he said as he handed the box to Andrew

He opened it with frank curiosity, only to discover a roll of parchment closely covered with equations. "What…?"

"Our system of mathematics is somewhat different from yours," Orestes explained. "But," he added with a wave of his hand, "I have no doubt you will figure it out. This small sample, by the way, deals with our major energy source.''

With proper care, Andrew rerolled the parchment and placed it back in the box. Holding it firmly, he rose to go. "Thank you, sir. I'll see that it's put to good use.''

"Fine, my boy, fine. Nothing's too good for a member of the family, after all. And perhaps one day you'll be able to return the favor."

"Of course," Andrew said automatically as he took his leave, his mind already filled with enticing visions of what the future would bring.

Epilogue

"I wish I'd known what he was thinking of," Andrew mused. He was lying on a lounge chair on the patio, looking out over the sea. It was late in the afternoon, and the shadows of the fading sun softened his features.

He was very tired, but then, that seemed to go with the territory these days. With a smile, he glanced down at the small bundle in his arms, the beloved cause of his fatigue.

"Orestes is a nice name," Marina countered as she watched the pair with loving eyes. She had known Andrew was a good father. Seeing him with Billy had told her that. But she hadn't expected him to prove so adept with a baby. It still startled her that he was better at changing diapers and giving baths than she was, but at least she was learning quickly.

Her husband raised his eyebrows. "For a girl?"

Marina's smile deepened. "All right, I admit that's

a bit unusual. But lots of people give a child a middle name that runs in the family. Jessica Orestes Paxton. It has a ring to it.''

Andrew glanced down at the tiny baby, who was fast asleep. Her lower lip drooped slightly, and her eyes were squinched up, as though concentrating on some scene only she could see. Resting up, he thought wryly, for the coming night. ''It's too big for her,'' he murmured.

''What is?''

''The name. She'll never grow into it.''

Marina laughed softly. Two weeks after the birth of their daughter, she felt surprisingly well. But then, her labor had been relatively swift. She had intended to return to Atlantis for the delivery, still feeling more comfortable with the doctors there. But Jessica had taken them by surprise, arriving two weeks early. They had barely made it to the hospital on St. John's in time for her appearance. She could still remember every moment of the wild ride, with the *Sea Witch* bucking a heavy swell and the wind crying in the fully rigged sails. ''Oh, I rather suspect she will,'' she said.

''We could have waited. Our next child might be a boy.''

''Orestes was impatient. Besides, he said he suspected I would bear only daughters out of sheer stubbornness.''

''Poor guy,'' Andrew said with mock sympathy. ''He had quite a shock when he discovered that women here are serious about equality.''

''He had an even bigger shock when the idea caught on so fast down there. Of course, Theseus's friend had something to do with that.''

''You mean Sybil?'' Andrew asked with a grin.

"She does seem to spend a lot of time there. A very devoted member of our delegation."

Marina stretched and lay back on her lounger. She could hear a dove cooing in the underbrush nearby. Billy was off visiting with Tristan, Cassia and their son, Austin. They would be bringing Billy home soon and would stay for dinner. Hildy had that firmly under control, so she could afford to relax and enjoy a peaceful interlude with her husband.

There had been few enough of those in the two years since their marriage. Barely had the week-long wedding celebration been concluded than they had been swept up by the demands of their two governments. To her considerable surprise, Marina had been appointed an emissary to the Outer World. Her uncle had made it clear that he was taking an enormous risk in naming a woman to such a position, particularly one who had already demonstrated a certain capacity for mischief. She knew with quiet confidence that she had proven more than worthy of his trust.

Meanwhile, Andrew had juggled both his duties as a representative of his own country and his efforts to decipher the equations Orestes had given him. Work on them had been completed only a few weeks before Jessica's birth. Within a very short time, the first of the new energy installations would be under construction with what were expected to be revolutionary effects.

"It must feel strange," she said as she reached out a hand to him, "to suddenly have nothing of great urgency to do."

"It's fine with me," he assured her, his gaze wandering over her tenderly. "I don't mind concentrating on my family. And in a few weeks...." He let the words trail off, his smile telling her what he was thinking.

She flushed slightly as desire stirred within her. Their lovemaking had been magnificent during her pregnancy, but they had stopped as a precaution several weeks before Jessica was born when Marina's doctor warned that she might come early. It would be a month or so before they could fully resume the delights their marriage had only refined. Anticipation gave a keen edge to their hunger for each other.

To distract herself, Marina said, "When I talked with Cassia this morning, she mentioned that there was something she and Tristan wanted to discuss with us. Do you have any idea what that might be?"

Before he could reply, Jessica stirred and began to cry. Her father handed her to her mother, who nestled her tenderly against her breast. As the baby began to nurse, Andrew laughed. "She's voracious. I don't know how you keep up with her."

"It's all right," Marina said softly, her eyes on the child. "I'm happy to do it. Besides, she's growing so fast. This time will be over before we know it."

He nodded slowly. "I've been meaning to talk with you about that. It has to do with what Tristan and Cassia want to discuss. Do you think Jessica will be old enough to travel soon?"

"I don't see why not. She's perfectly healthy. If you mean taking her to Atlantis...."

"There's that, of course. Your family's been very patient, but it won't last much longer. We'll have to let them meet her. But what I had in mind was something else that's more...ambitious."

At her raised eyebrows, he smiled almost sheepishly.

"You know those books Billy has about King Arthur and the Knights of the Round Table?"

"I should think so, since those are the only bedtime stories he wants to hear."

"Well...it seems Tristan has this idea..."

"Don't tell me," she said. "He wants to look for Camelot."

"Not exactly. You see, the legend says that after Arthur died, he was taken away to a place called Avalon, where he was cared for by people who were highly skilled in magic. Tristan and I were talking about it not too long ago, and we decided that Avalon just might have something to do with the other group of survivors from Atlantis."

She thought about that for a moment, then said slowly, "It sounds unbelievable, but I have to admit, there could be a chance that you're right."

"Care to find out?"

The dove cooed again, and high overhead the first stars began to appear, all but invisible against the pale sky. She stroked the baby's silken cheek and thought of how far her dreams had already taken her.

With a smile, she met her husband's gaze. "I don't see any reason to stop now," she said.

* * * * *

INTIMATE MOMENTS™

is proud to present

Romancing the Crown

*With the help of their powerful allies,
the royal family of Montebello is determined
to find their missing heir. But the search for the
beloved prince is not without danger—or passion!*

**This exciting twelve-book series begins in January and
continues throughout the year with these fabulous titles:**

Available at your favorite retail outlet.

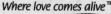

Silhouette®

Where love comes alive™